THE GREAT
SKINNER STRIKE

THE GREAT SKINNER STRIKE

STEPHANIE S. TOLAN

MACMILLAN PUBLISHING CO., INC.
New York

Macmillan Publishing Co., Inc.
866 Third Avenue, New York, N.Y. 10022
Collier Macmillan Canada, Inc.
Printed in the United States of America
10 9 8 7 6 5 4 3 2 1

Library of Congress Cataloging in Publication Data
Tolan, Stephanie S.
The great Skinner strike.
Summary: When fourteen-year-old Jenny Skinner's
mother goes on strike for better working conditions
in the home, and as a result polarizes much of their
community, Jenny, her three younger siblings, and her
father come to some surprising conclusions.
[1. Strikes and lockouts—Fiction.   2. Mothers—
Fiction.   3. Women's rights—Fiction]   I. Title.
PZ7.T5735Gre   1983   [Fic]   82-17992
ISBN 0-02-789360-X

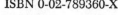

To Letty Cottin Pogrebin
(who makes it sound almost easy)
and to Bob, Bob Jr., Pat, Andy and RJ Tolan
(who remind me that it isn't)

CONTENTS

BEGINNING

We're not telling this story to get
famous. Fame isn't all it's cracked up to
be. We're telling it because nobody has
given our side. They told _her_ side, from
one end of the country to the other. They
told _his_ side. But if they even mentioned
us, it was only to prove something they
wanted to prove. Reporters ought to get
out of journalism and into fiction. We
decided, Rick and Marcia and Ben and I,
to tell it from the kids' point of view.
I, Jenny Skinner, was chosen to do the
telling because a) I'm fourteen and the
oldest; b) I get A's in English; and c)
nobody else wanted to do it.

When it all started, the Skinner family
was an ordinary middle-class family,
larger than average—with four kids—but
not a tribe or anything. We aren't rich
and we aren't poor. Dad is a middle-range
executive in a medium-size company. We
have two cars, one of them old, and three

televisions, one of them black and white
and <u>very</u> small. We have meat with every
dinner because Dad insists on it, but the
meat is often hamburger and more often
chicken. There's a lot of moaning about
inflation, especially in late August when
everybody has to have shoes and clothes
for school, and in the middle of winter,
when the heating bills are at their worst.

Mom is a normal, middle-class woman. I
mean she <u>was</u>. She didn't fit any of the
stereotypes, like the woman with the
housedress and apron, or the one with the
unshaved armpits and jeans, or the one
with the three-piece suit and brief case.
She was just a person, like the rest of
us. She was nice some of the time and
grumpy some of the time. She took care of
her kids and the house and was president
of the PTA. She worked part-time as a
research librarian. She could help us
with homework because she'd had a good
education and she could fish and chop
firewood because she'd camped out a lot
when she was a kid. In the fourteen years
I have known her she has been dependable.
She could be counted on to go crazy and
yell at us if we got too loud in the house
and she could be counted on to come through
if anybody needed last-minute cookies for
a bake sale. We knew her pretty well. Or
we thought we did.

The earthquake which is supposed to dump California into the ocean sometime soon couldn't be any worse than the shock that brought our ordinariness crashing down around us the first week in October. There was a fault line in the Skinner family, but nobody knew it—except Mom.

I could have called what you've just read the "Foreword," but I was afraid you wouldn't read it. Now I'll get to the story itself, starting at what was for <u>us</u> the beginning—Monday, October 3.

DAY ONE

It was sunny. It was one of those days that make you think of football or hayrides or apples. I remember that I wore a jacket to school in the morning because it was too cold to wait for the bus in just jeans and a tee-shirt, but that after school it was too warm for the jacket. That's why Rick, who's eight years old and the "baby," forgot and left his jacket at school again. Rick always has to have three times as many jackets and lunch boxes and gym sneakers as anybody else because he's always leaving them someplace.

I think the weather is important because if it had been fifty-five and raining, Mom might not have done what she did. Marcia, who is ten and very realistic, says bad weather would just have postponed it. She's probably right. But on Day One, I preferred to think Mom had gotten the idea from watching the Donahue show in the morning and, if she hadn't been able to follow through that very day, might have forgotten the whole thing by suppertime.

Ben was first to discover the New Mom. He's nearly thirteen and wouldn't have been the first one home that day except that he'd tried to jump down the whole first flight of stairs outside Fair Oaks Junior High and had hurt his ankle, so he couldn't go to soccer practice. Actually, he could have gone just to watch, but he was embarrassed for anyone to know what he'd done. He's not too old to *do* childish things, he's just too old to admit doing them. Ben is very sensitive about appearances. (That's why no one is allowed to say he's twelve. He's been saying he's "almost thirteen" since two days after his birthday.)

Anyway, Ben was hobbling down the street from the bus stop, trying to decide whether he should go for sympathy and make sure his limp was noticeable (at the risk of being laughed at for how it happened) or whether he should be noble and courageous and play down the pain. He had just realized that playing down the pain wouldn't get him any sympathy, and had increased his limp, when he passed the Andersons' hedge and saw *her*. He was so surprised that he forgot his injury altogether. There was *our mother*, walking up and down in our front yard, carrying a placard that said "ON STRIKE, UNFAIR LABOR PRACTICES."

The first thing he did was to jump back behind the hedge. He needed time to think about what he'd seen and to be sure no one had seen *him*. There wasn't anyone out on the block in either direction, so he risked peeking around the bushes. She was really there, walking back and forth, stopping at each end of her route to switch her placard so that the words would still be visible from the street. The placard was tacked to a sponge mop, whose dirty yellow sponge was obviously supposed to be part of the message.

Ben considered his options. He couldn't stay where he was, because people would be coming home from school or work soon and he was not about to be seen there. He couldn't go to his friend Mark's house because Mark was at soccer practice. And obviously, he couldn't hide in the Andersons' hedge. Already he was feeling as if people were watching from all the windows in the neighborhood—watching and laughing. Since an awful lot of people in our neighborhood work during the day, that feeling was silly, but he couldn't help it. The only thing to do was to go around the back and get inside the house.

What he saw when he got to our backyard was even more surprising than Mom picketing in the front. The back door was closed and probably locked. But it wouldn't have mattered whether it was locked or not, because there were two pieces of two-by-four nailed across it. Nailed! Right into the wood trim that Mom had painted only last spring. He recognized the boards as leftovers from the go-cart he'd made, so he knew she'd taken them from his workshop in the garage. The nails had come from there too. They were the largest nails he had, and they'd been hammered in very neatly and very firmly. The longer he stood looking at that boarded-up door, the madder he got. He wasn't going to be shut out of his own house, with his own boards and nails, so he went around to the basement window behind the forsythia bush—the one with the broken catch. It was boarded from the inside. None of the first-floor windows could be opened because the storm windows latched on the inside, and the storms were down. The extension ladder wouldn't do any good either because the same was true on the second floor. Czar Nicholas, our large gray Persian cat, was sitting on the kitchen window sill looking smug, apparently unaware that he was a prisoner. Ben could hear Buffy, our half–golden retriever, barking inside, but he couldn't see her. Probably she was waiting behind the door for him to come in. She'd have to wait a long time, he thought.

Ben was beginning to imagine eyes on him again. He slipped around the side of the house to check on Mom. He

hoped he'd had a hallucination before. But she was there,
all right, still walking back and forth with her placard. On
this side, the placard was a green Magic Marker map of
Pennsylvania with a red star for Harrisburg. Ben recognized
it as Rick's social studies project from last spring. There were
other things he hadn't noticed before. On one side of the
front yard, under the big oak tree, our tent was pitched.
Next to it was the picnic table, protected by the canvas fly
we use when we go camping. Under the table was our big
camping icebox and on it were the Coleman stove and
lantern. Another sign, made of cardboard from the back of
a legal pad, was hanging on the canopy at the front of the
tent, but he could only see the back of it, so he didn't know
at the time that it said "Strike Headquarters." He didn't care
what it said. He went to the garage.

Rick got home next. He didn't pay any attention to Mom's
sign or the strangeness of our tent on the front lawn. He just
went and asked for his after-school snack. She told him she
didn't have anything to offer him. When he found the door
locked and discovered that he couldn't get inside to the
refrigerator, he cried. But Mom, who is usually so soft-
hearted with Rick that one little whimper gets him practically anything he wants, didn't turn a hair. She went right
on walking back and forth as if she didn't hear him. After a
while, he gave up and went to sit on the front steps.

   Marcia, who got there a few minutes later, went to ask
Mom what was going on. When Mom wouldn't pay any more
attention to her than she had to Rick, Marcia tried to go in
the front door, and was the first to find out that Mom had
thrown the deadbolt. Even with her key, she couldn't get in.

   I got home last. That's because my friend Sarah and I had

gone to the library to do some research in case John Bertoni
and Tim Reardon, who go to the library a lot, happened to
be there. (They were, but they were too busy to notice us.
Sarah says they were faking.) When I arrived Marcia was
walking up and down with Mom, trying to get her to explain. Rick was still sitting on the steps, sniffling a little and
trying to look starved. Any lingering thoughts about John
Bertoni were driven right out of my mind.

I happen to be a worrier. Even when there's nothing much
to worry about, I can concoct mental pictures that would
give a yogi stress headaches. The scene in our front yard
provided me with lots of material. My first mental picture
was full of men in white coats taking Mom away and leaving
us "poor motherless children." The next version had the men
taking me away because I'd imagined the whole thing.
Finally, when Marcia told me we couldn't get into the house,
I imagined social workers coming to take us all to foster
homes where we'd be kept in attic rooms and fed nothing
but bread crusts. For some reason, in all my imaginings, I
seem to have forgotten Dad. It must have been the shock of
the moment.

It's hard to explain how I felt, standing in my front yard,
my arms full of books, watching my own mother walk a
picket line in front of our locked-up house. Basically the
feeling was almost-terminal embarrassment. Sometimes,
when I go to the grocery with Mom, she'll start to talk to
the check-out person. I remember one time she told this
perfect stranger that she was buying Raisin Bran because
all four of her kids would eat it and it kept her from having
to buy prune juice or Ex-Lax. I wanted to be clear on the
other side of the store so people would think I'd never seen
that woman before. I felt like that now, only worse. Much

worse. Marcia told me to take a turn trying to talk to Mom, but I just couldn't. From the hammering in the garage, I could tell that Ben was in his workshop. I figured he was working on the solar heating project he'd stopped when the soccer season began, but later he admitted he'd been too upset to work, so was only pretending. He was sitting on his workbench, randomly smacking it with a hammer.

Eventually, people began to get home. Everybody in our neighborhood drives to work. The only people who walk anywhere are kids and old Mrs. Haggeman, who goes to the grocery store with one of those little fold-up carts. So the end of the work day didn't bring a whole crowd of people on foot. Instead, it tied up traffic. Cars that usually zip right by were creeping along at about three miles an hour so the drivers could gawk at the spectacle in our front yard. It was like being in the center ring at the circus. Soon, I knew, would come all those joggers who went out before dinner. They were bound to have trouble keeping up to speed when they passed our house. I began to imagine the whole town gathering to watch the crazy housewife on strike.

Then I remembered Dad. It was a great relief. He'd be home any minute and I was certain that his arrival would mean the end of this horrible charade. As it happened, I was wrong.

It wasn't that he didn't try to stop it—he did. But carefully. Both Mom and Dad believe that parents should present a united front to their children. They're supposed to be a team. So he didn't jump out of the car and start yelling, as some men might have. I want to say here and now that he behaved with admirable restraint, considering that the traffic snarl had added fifteen minutes to the time it usually took him to get home, and considering that when he did get

there, his own wife turned out to be causing the snarl. He pulled into the driveway, stopped the car, and just sat for a minute, taking it all in. By this time there were a couple of kids standing around watching, besides the cars creeping by. Dad shook his head once or twice, either trying to deny what he saw or trying to clear his vision. Then he got out of the car and walked over to Mom to have what he probably thought would be a short, whispered conversation. I think he expected to be discreet and firm and effective. His first trouble was that Mom didn't stop walking. After a couple of whispered words, he had to run after her so she could hear what he was saying. He stopped walking when he finished and waited for an answer, but she just kept on until she reached her usual turning place, shifted her sign, and walked right back past him again. Then she paused long enough to say something very short, in which the only word I could hear was, not surprisingly, "strike," and then she continued. Dad followed her through one-half her circuit, talking quietly and calmly. Again she went on without answering.

He stopped, shrugged his shoulders, and went up the steps, patting Rick on the head as he passed him, and tried to open the front door. When it didn't open, he fished his keys out of his pocket to unlock it. That's when he found out about the deadbolt. I was very impressed with his calm. He nonchalantly put his keys back into his pocket, turned, and came down the walk to where I was standing. "What do you know about this?" he asked quietly.

"Nothing."

"Is it some kind of joke?"

I shook my head. "It doesn't seem very funny to me," I said. I had just thought of the possibility that John Bertoni

might for some reason pass our house on his way home from the library. If he did that, I would die. Right there on the sidewalk.

"The back door's locked too," Marcia announced. "And boarded up." Dad just looked at her. "Two-by-fours nailed across it," Marcia assured him. "Honest."

Rick joined us then. "I'm starving!" He looked as if he might be working up to crying again, but Dad didn't wait for him to start. This time, when Dad spoke to Mom, he was no longer playing the role of united-front parent and teammate. This time he stood directly in her path, and this time she stopped and listened. Then she answered. They both kept their voices very low, so we couldn't hear what they were saying. Pretty soon they were both talking about as much with their hands as with their voices, and as their gestures grew larger and faster, we could sort of tell what they meant. Dad was suggesting that Mom had gone mad, and she was indicating both sanity and determination. He wanted to know about boarded-up doors and she insisted on her right to board them. By this time, the first of the joggers had joined the group of kids. So had Mrs. Haggeman, without her grocery cart. Then Mrs. Anderson came around her hedge to get her three-year-old daughter Amy, who had wandered over. Mrs. Anderson stayed to watch. Dad seemed to realize that he had an audience. He spoke to Mom once more, in a very few words, stepped out of her way, and started toward us again. Mother continued her circuit as if the conversation had never taken place.

"Get Ben now, Rick," Dad said, his voice loud and hearty. "We're off to Burger King!" The tone of his voice seemed to indicate that this trip to Burger King had been planned for a long time. I don't think anybody was fooled, though. After Rick's initial whoop of joy, he went off toward the garage at a run. He was back almost immediately, alone.

"He's not coming out," he said. "He says to bring him a bacon burger and fries and a chocolate shake. He says please get the boards off the door before dark because then he's going to come out of the garage and go straight to his room."

Dad smiled a big smile in Mrs. Anderson's direction and ruffled Rick's hair. "Of course Ben can keep working," he said loudly. "We can't interrupt a scientist." He started for the car. "Come on, kids!" he called with hearty good cheer. "If we don't hurry, we'll be late!"

Rick started to ask, "Late for what?" but Marcia, who understood, punched him in the arm and he shut up.

After dinner, when we couldn't put it off any longer, we went home to see if Mom had changed her mind. As we'd all expected, she hadn't. I began to wonder if she ever intended to sit down. We couldn't tell if she'd eaten or not, because everything looked the same. Probably she was going to wait until dark when nobody would be able to read her sign any more. Luckily, the spectators had all gone away. Even the strange sight of a woman picketing in front of her own house isn't enough to keep most people from their dinners. Marcia took Ben's food into the garage. He'd quit hammering by this time and was doing his math.

Dad tried talking to Mom again, but the results were the same as before. So there we were, as it got colder and the sun began to go down, gathered around the car in our driveway, wondering what to do next. Dad really didn't want to pry the boards off the back door. It was the principle of the thing, he told us. "She's going to get tired of all this, and it's going to get cold out here tonight. Maybe by tomorrow, she'll decide to give it up. We could spend the night at the Econolodge over by I-67."

"What'll we wear to school tomorrow?" I asked. "Our clothes are inside."

Marcia frowned. "Anyway, we have to get in tonight. Buffy's in there, and if we don't let her out, she's going to pee all over the carpet."

So Rick got the crowbar from the garage and Dad pried the boards off the door. When we opened it, Buffy didn't even stop to say hello. She rushed straight out, squatted at her favorite spot next to the fence, and then ran around the house to the very person who had locked her inside in the first place. Buffy had joined the strike. We didn't know then that she was to be only the first of many.

THE DAY AFTER

Our mother's full name is Eleanor Jean Woodford Skinner. She is called Ellie. If "Ellie" sounds to you like a name for someone little and cute, you're right in this case. She's five feet three inches tall, weighs under 110 pounds, and has a very young face. Her hair is dark brown, with a few streaks of gray, and she wears it very short and sort of wavy. On the day she began her strike she was thirty-eight, "old enough to know better," Ben said. Little as she is, Ellie Skinner is not fragile. She spent two weeks by herself in a wilderness area in Montana when she was eighteen, so why Dad thought she'd be put off by a chilly night in a tent in Pennsylvania, I don't know. Wishful thinking, I guess. By the time people were up and around and going off to work the next morning, she was back on her picket line, dressed in jeans and a plaid wool shirt, walking up and down with her placard and a mug of hot coffee. Buffy trailed along at her heels. The weather was holding and so were they.

Looking at the situation from the outside, it would seem that Ellie Skinner had it pretty good. Dad's a nice person who doesn't drink and doesn't hang around with "the guys." He doesn't spend every weekend golfing or hunting or anything like that. And we're decent enough as kids go. Some of us are kind of messy, it's true, but there's nobody on drugs or pregnant or in trouble with the police or anything like that. Mom didn't have to be "just a housewife" because she had a job she liked, even if it didn't pay as much as she thought it should. So on the morning of October 4, we couldn't figure it out. Dad thought it might be a midlife crisis of some kind. Since he's forty, *he* was actually the one who was supposed to be having problems, he said. Women are supposed to have theirs earlier, so Mom should have been through that already.

Whether it was a midlife crisis or not, Dad thought she would probably get over it. He pointed out that living in a tent on the front lawn couldn't be much fun for very long, especially since there were certain obvious inconveniences.

"All I know is that I'm not going to go out there where people can see me," Ben said. "If you can't make Mom come in, I want a ride to school. I don't want any of the guys to know this has anything to do with me." If Ben had known that even as he spoke there were photographers outside taking pictures of Mom and Buffy looking "cute," I don't know what he would have done. He still thought he could avoid being associated with Mom just by staying out of sight.

Marcia was thinking of more practical matters. Mom had chosen to begin her strike at a strategic time. We were virtually out of clean clothes, since Monday was laundry day. It was now Tuesday, grocery day, so there wasn't much in the house to eat, unless someone could figure out what was in all those foil-wrapped packages in the freezer. By the time we'd all put milk on our Cheerios, the milk was gone. In fact, Rick was complaining that because he was last, he'd had to eat his cereal practically dry. Ben and I always ate lunch in the cafeteria at school, but Marcia and Rick carried their lunches. She announced that the two slices of bread and the slightly blackened banana she'd found were not going to make much of a lunch for the two of them. Rick managed to find an unopened box of Granola bars, but neither of them was very happy at the prospect of a lunch that consisted of one piece of peanut-buttered bread, a Granola bar, and half an overripe banana.

Despite the growing evidence that the situation was bordering on tragedy, Dad would not budge from his determination to Ignore the Strike.

"She isn't going to be able to stick it out for long," he said. "We can outlast her."

I wasn't so sure. "What about the coal miners?" I asked.

"What coal miners? What about them?"

"The companies thought they could starve the union out, but then they realized that coal companies have to have coal."

"It isn't the same thing," Dad said.

"And what about printers? There've been printers' unions that went on strike and drove whole newspapers right out of existence."

"It isn't the same thing," Dad repeated. "We aren't a company. And your mother isn't a union. She's just one person."

I had a feeling that even though she was just one person, a strike that cut off "essential services" couldn't safely be ignored. "We don't even know what she wants yet. Shouldn't we at least try to find out?"

"Before dinnertime," Rick said.

"We should at least find out if we can give her what she wants," Marcia said.

"The main thing is to get her to stop! Right now!" Ben said.

Dad stood up, pushed his chair against the kitchen table

so hard the Cheerios box fell over, and squashed his napkin into a tight ball. (He hadn't had any coffee that morning.) "Your mother has everything a woman could reasonably ask for. She has a husband, a loving family, enough money, a job, and a fine home! This is a breakfast table, not a bargaining table." He checked his watch. "Ben, I'm leaving. If you're in the car when I back out, you'll get your ride. If not, you won't!" His exit was only a little marred by the fact that he had to come back for his keys, which he'd left by his cereal bowl. As I picked up the box, I remembered that Dad hates Cheerios.

After Dad and Ben left, Marcia put the meager lunches into her and Rick's lunch boxes, made sure Rick had his backpack and another jacket, and shoved him out the back door. He has to leave earlier than she does because he tends to get sidetracked on his way to school. Even leaving early, he's late sometimes. Then she rushed around and put the bowls into the sink and the empty milk carton in the trash. "Look at the way they left things," she complained. "If this thing doesn't get settled fast, the health department will come down on us, wait and see!"

After Marcia left, I gathered up my books and stood for a few minutes, looking around the kitchen. Marcia was right —but who had time to clean up after breakfast? None of us. Czar Nicholas rubbed against my legs and meowed pitifully. Nobody had fed him. And there was nobody left in the house but me.

That's why I had to practically run all the way to the bus stop. Sarah was already there when I arrived, but luckily the bus wasn't in sight yet. I needed to tell Sarah what was happening. She, like Marcia, is not a worrier. She doesn't panic when things are going wrong. She looks at the situation carefully, decides what to do, and does it. What I needed from her was sympathy. And after that, what I needed was advice.

Since she is my closest friend, you'd think I would have remembered something else about Sarah that morning in particular. Sarah is a rabid feminist. She does things like keeping a record of TV commercials to see which are the most sexist, and then writing letters to the companies. Her parents got a divorce when Sarah was six and her sister Mimi was eight, probably because her mother, who always takes everything to extremes, had gotten her consciousness raised so high she couldn't live with a man any more. Since then the three of them have lived in an all-female household being blatantly independent. Her mother supports them by working at a bank and Sarah can hardly even remember what her father looks like. If I had been thinking rationally about all this, I would have realized that Sarah might not be the best source of sympathy. But it was not a time for thinking rationally, it was a time for needing friends. So I told her.

"Fantastic!" she said. "A strike! That's fantastic!"

I thought about Rick's and Marcia's pitiful lunches. "What's so fantastic?" I asked.

"That she's actually *doing* it. I can't wait to tell Rachel." One of Sarah's liberations is that she calls her mother by her first name. That's supposed to make her mother a person instead of a title. "It's almost too bad my father isn't around any more. I'll bet Rachel would join the strike in a minute, if she had anybody to strike against."

Right then and there I knew that Sarah didn't understand what was going on. This strike wasn't just against Dad. It was against *us*. All of us. While Sarah and I were standing there on the corner, Sarah could be sure that at home her dresser drawers were full of clean underwear. And at dinner time, she'd have a nice, hot meal that didn't come from Burger King. Sarah did not fully grasp our plight.

"We could honor the picket line," she mused.

"Honor the picket line? You're supposed to sleep over Friday night." I hoped it wouldn't last that long.

"That's okay. We'll just change it to our house. Rachel won't mind. She'll want to help your mom any way she can. Ooh, Jenny," she said, hugging her books to herself. "Aren't you proud?"

No, I thought. It wasn't the only thing I thought. But the arrival of our bus saved me from answering and losing a friend.

That evening, the Skinner family was dealt several hard blows. The first one was delivered with the evening paper. On the front page of the Family Living section, taking up over half the page, was a picture of Mom with the sponge mop sign. Buffy was in the picture, too. The headline read, "Homemaker on Strike." That was pretty straightforward, factual, and unbiased. But under it was an article written by the editor of the Family Living section (a woman) that made Mom sound like a cross between Annie Oakley and Joan of Arc. By contrast, the rest of the Skinner family looked like greedy and ungrateful parasites. The reporter's version of our family was that we were a bunch of lazy good-for-nothings who came home every day to be waited on by poor Mom, who'd been slaving away half the day in the house to clean and cook and do our laundry and the other half the day at the library. According to the story, Mom's part-time job was actually a *career* that had to take a back seat to all the other work Mom did, caring for her

children and husband and mopping the kitchen floor. Buffy was the only member of the family who cared enough to stand by Poor Mom the Martyr. There was even a bit about Mom's wilderness living "before she accepted the burden of family life," and her willingness to "rough it" on the front lawn to make her point. By the time I finished reading it, I was ready to throw up. Whatever happened to apple pie and motherhood?

Dad read the article with all the enthusiasm of a movie star reading one of those grocery store newspapers. He kept grumbling about libel and bias and yellow journalism. Ben took one look at the picture, saw that the article mentioned our names, and went straight back to the garage. He spent the whole rest of the evening out there, hammering like a madman, which is how he managed to miss the second blow.

It came with a phone call. The phone had been ringing pretty regularly since just after the newspaper came, and almost everyone had wanted to speak to Mom. Those were the "we're with you" calls Dad dealt with by announcing that Ellie Skinner didn't have a phone, as far as he knew. But this call was different. The others had been from strangers. When Dad picked up the receiver this time, ready to snap at whoever was on the other end of the line, he had to bite back his reaction. It was the head librarian—Mom's boss. "I'm sorry, Mrs. Stephenson," Dad said, "but she isn't here. Perhaps someone could take her a message." He listened then, and there was nothing all that spectacular about his reaction to what he heard. He just blinked a few times, very rapidly, like a bullfrog swallowing a cricket. "She'll call you," he said in a tight voice. Then he put down the receiver so hard it bounced right off the phone again and dangled at the end of its cord, banging against the wall. Rick, who was

eating some stale potato chips he'd found in the back of a cupboard, hung up the phone. Marcia and I just looked at Dad. The expression on his face didn't invite questions.

"Your mother has quit her job," he said finally.

Marcia looked at me and shrugged. It didn't seem like much of a catastrophe to *us*. After all, if she had quit doing the jobs around the house that affected us all so seriously (we'd had fish and chips for dinner this time), why should we care that she'd quit a job that didn't affect us at all? It just goes to show how little we knew about the functioning of our own family. It had never occurred to us that Mom's job, which she always complained paid too little for the time and work it involved, had anything to do with the way we lived. We didn't think about the possibility that several thousand dollars suddenly removed from our yearly budget would hurt. Dad, of course, understood immediately.

I think it was that second blow more than anything else that changed Dad's mind about ignoring the strike. People try to pretend money isn't important, or isn't as important as other things. But underneath it all, they know better.

The rest of the blows that evening were minor. Mostly the phone rang with calls Dad didn't want to take. The ones from the women who wanted to support Mom he didn't even deal with. He just hung up. The ones offering him sympathy—also from women—he was polite about. But the worst, judging from his visibly rising blood pressure, were from men who wanted to know how he could "allow" his wife to behave that way. After the third of those, he announced he was going to 7-Eleven to pick up enough groceries to keep us from starving. As soon as he left, we took the phone off the hook. We didn't want to talk to any of those people.

It was probably a whole night of lying on his side of the otherwise empty king-size bed, thinking about the loss of Mom's paycheck, that took Dad out to the picnic table the next morning in a fair imitation of a reasonable mood, even without his morning coffee. (He'd forgotten to buy any and Mom had let it run out before she went on strike.)

At the risk of missing my bus, I went with him. I had to wear the same tee-shirt I'd worn the day before, so I felt I had a stake in the negotiations. When Mom offered Dad a seat at the picnic table, I sat down next to him.

"Good morning, Eleanor," he said. I thought it was a reasonable opening, if a little formal.

"Good morning, Mike." Mom was incredibly cheerful for a person who had spent two nights on the cold ground and had been without a bathroom all that time. She was still looking "cute" in her plaid wool shirt.

"I think it's time we talked about this," Dad said.

"I think so." She smiled. It did not seem to be the smile of a crazy person.

There was a long pause. Dad was staring off toward the Andersons' hedge, apparently waiting for Mom to begin. She didn't. She just looked at him expectantly, still smiling. When he finally realized she wasn't going to speak first, he cleared his throat and looked in her direction, but slightly past her right ear. "Would you like to explain exactly what this strike is all about?" His tone had lost its determined reasonableness. It bordered on hostility.

Mom's smile vanished. "Am I supposed to believe that you don't know?"

Dad looked directly at her very briefly, before his eyes slid back to the space beside her ear. "Have I missed something? Did you leave a list of demands somewhere?"

Mom shook her head. "It's worse than I thought," she said, almost to herself. Another long pause. The late crickets were chirping in the tall tufts of grass by the front steps and some sparrows were fussing in the bushes under the living room window. Neither of them spoke. I'd expected just to listen to the negotiations, but there wasn't anything to listen to, so I decided I could talk. "*What's* worse than you thought?" I asked. "And what did you think?"

Mom looked at me and shook her head again. "I knew I could say a lot around here without being heard, but I did think somebody heard some of it. Some of the time. At least the most important things."

Before I had a chance to ask what these important things were that nobody had heard, Dad decided to say something. "Why did you quit your job?" he asked.

It wasn't a question I cared about, but I wasn't in charge of the meeting, so I had to sit there, wondering what Mom had been saying that we hadn't been hearing. Mom laughed. "I thought that would get your attention," she said.

Dad snorted. Then he stood up. "You quit your job to get my attention?"

"I haven't managed to any other way."

"I would appreciate having your demands in writing," he said, "so nobody can say I didn't hear them." No more pretense about being cool and reasonable. I noticed for the first time the aroma of fresh coffee coming from the end of the table where the stove was. Mom had made a mistake, I realized. If she'd wanted a rational bargaining session she should have offered him coffee. Too late. The session, such as it had been, was obviously over. Dad stalked off toward the house.

I didn't know what to do. Mom smiled at me, but I didn't

smile back. I knew for sure I wasn't on her side and I didn't want her to think I was. I got up and followed Dad. I'd missed the school bus by this time, so he'd have to give me a ride to school anyway.

Ben announced when we were back in the kitchen that he wasn't going to school that day. He was going to be an "almost-thirteen-year-old dropout." It was a clear sign of Dad's mental state that he didn't argue the point.

THE NINETY-FIVE THESES

That really isn't an accurate or even a fair title, but don't blame me. That's what Mom called the sheet of paper she tacked up on our front door while we were away at school/work/garage that day. For those of you who are neither Lutherans nor history buffs, I should tell you that the Ninety-five Theses were what Martin Luther nailed up on a church door when the Reformation was beginning. Up till that time, there was the Catholic Church. Martin Luther and the Reformation introduced the world to Protestants. Ben says that's a serious oversimplification, so I'll admit here and now that I'm neither a Lutheran nor a history buff myself. I just thought I should explain at least a little of what Mom meant when she chose that title for her demands. Martin Luther and people like him changed the course of history. This was Mom's subtle way of telling us that she was after something bigger than we'd thought.

When we got home, several changes had taken place in our situation. This was obvious to everyone except Ben, who refused to come around to the front of the house to notice anything. The "Strike Headquarters" sign over the tent had taken on a new meaning. There were bunches of women in our front yard, going in and out of the tent, sitting at the picnic table, even walking Mom's up-till-then solitary picket line. A woman dressed in an alligator shirt and wraparound skirt was walking right next to Mom, talking to her about a mile a minute. I knew she couldn't be an interviewer because she wasn't letting Mom get a word in. All Mom was doing was nodding from time to time.

Sarah had come home with me to see what was happening. I was doing my best to tolerate Sarah's enthusiasm because she was my friend. But it wasn't easy. When we arrived, Marcia was sitting against a tree, writing on a steno pad. Rick, she said, had gone to his friend Joey's house because Joey had one of those cookie-baking mothers.

"What is all this?" I asked.

"Spreading fires!" Sarah said. I refrained from pointing out that I was speaking to my sister.

"What are you doing?" This question was clearly meant for Marcia.

"I'm taking notes. My teacher said I could write an extra-credit report on the strike. This mess might as well do me some good, as long as I'm stuck in the middle of it!"

"Who are all these people?"

"Don't you recognize some of them? There's Mrs. Secrist. And Mrs. Apple and Mrs. Thomas. You won't believe it, but Mrs. Anderson was here when I got home. With Amy."

"Why shouldn't I believe it? What's going on?"

"Spreading fires," Sarah said again, her voice fairly dripping with enthusiasm. I just glared at her.

"They're starting an organization," Marcia said.

"Like a union? A real union? What'll it be, United Mother Workers? The American Federation of Housewives?"

"Sort of like that."

Buffy was leaning against the blue-jeaned legs of a woman at the end of the picnic bench. While the woman talked to another woman next to her, she was scratching Buffy's ears. "A union of mothers and dogs," I said to nobody in particular. "Wonderful." I turned to ask Sarah if she'd changed her mind about coming into the house, but she wasn't next to me any more. She was halfway to the tent. "Terrific," I said to her back. "Join them!" I wondered where she thought she'd fit—with the mothers or with the dogs.

"What's that big sheet of paper on the door?" I asked Marcia.

"The Ninety-five Theses. Mom's demands."

"She's got ninety-five demands?" I didn't know about Martin Luther then.

Marcia shook her head. "There aren't really ninety-five. Just six. The title's like a joke, sort of. Something about Lutherans or something. Mom started to tell me, but that lady interrupted. Go read it for yourself."

So I did. This is what I read:

THE NINETY-FIVE THESES
Preamble

As society changes, so does the family. Lower-class or rural American families traditionally required the active participation of each family member for survival. Willingly or unwillingly, family members participated. Wealthy families, on the other hand, maintained a staff of servants to meet practical needs, freeing family members to engage in other activities. Today, few families could afford servants even if there were enough people willing to spend their lives at such work. However, most middle-class families wish to live according to the standards of the wealthy of an earlier time. The most common effect of this expectation is to force one member, the mother, to become the servant of all other members. The Skinner family could serve as a textbook case of this sociological phenomenon.

In the beginning of this country there were slaves. It took a civil war to effect their emancipation. Next there were wage slaves. Unions, strikes, violence, and social upheaval were required to free the wage slaves from their corporate masters. Today there are "wives/ mothers" whose position in the patriarchal family is too often contemporary slavery.

I have gone on strike to call attention to this situation and to demand a "reformation" of the institution of the American family, beginning with the Skinners. The following demands must be met if a new, more humane, democratic, and just structure is to be created:

1. The position of "mother" shall have equal status in the family with "father" and "child."

2. Money shall not be the sole criterion for assessing the value of any member's contribution to family survival. Money is only one of many essentials for healthy and comfortable family life.

3. Each member of the family shall have both rights and responsibilities. Rights shall include the right to love, respect, food, shelter, clothing, and a reasonable amount of time and money to spend according to personal preference. Responsibilities shall include a share in providing those rights for each of the other members.

4. Each member shall be expected to contribute to the welfare of the family according to that member's abilities. Refusal to contribute fairly will abrogate that member's rights as defined above.

5. Grievances shall be discussed by the family as a whole, with all members afforded an equal opportunity to be heard.

6. No family policy shall be implemented which would require one family member to shoulder all burdens created by such a policy.

Until the Skinner family agrees to a reasonable discussion of the above demands, the undersigned, Eleanor Jean Woodford Skinner, will continue to absent herself and her services from the family unit.

I told you my mother was well educated. I had to go inside to look up "abrogate" to be sure it meant what I thought it meant. It did. Demand number four meant approximately that anyone who didn't help wouldn't eat. It was obvious that the sheet tacked up on our front door wasn't meant for our eyes alone. In fact, the one on the door was only the original. Copies had been distributed to newspapers, radio and television stations—even the wire services, via her newly acquired cohorts and agents. Their numbers were growing, even as I stood on the porch and read the demands.

By the time I was back with Marcia and her steno pad, Sarah was returning from the tent with a sheaf of copies in her hand, grinning. "This is great!" she said, "great!" She gave one to Marcia for her report, then tried to hand one to me. I shook my head. "I've read it."

I looked at my two-day-old shirt, thought about my nearly

empty dresser drawers, and forgot my intention to be tolerant of Sarah's attitude. "Let's go inside," I said to Marcia. "Certain people don't believe in crossing picket lines, and we need to talk." As Marcia and I started around the house toward the back door, I tossed a question in Sarah's general direction. "Who does the laundry at your house, Sarah— *you*?"

DEPRIVATION

Later that evening, our motherless group was sitting around the depressing remains of the frozen turkey roll Dad had heated for dinner, trying not to look at the bowl of red liquid and fruit cocktail that was supposed to have been Jell-O. (Did you know that fruit Jell-O can't be made in half an hour, even in the freezer?) We were up against the hard wall of reality. Mom was not coming inside. She was not going to take pity on us and come to our rescue. All afternoon, as people came and went outside, including more press people with more cameras, she resolutely ignored the members of the family. She ignored even Rick, who had tried his woeful puppy-dog face on her for half an hour! He had finally decided that she wasn't his mother at all, but a wicked stepmother. The Gypsies, he said, had stolen his real mother when he was a baby. He clung to this theory in spite of all attempts to point out its more unreasonable aspects. In view of dinner, it was hard not to understand how he felt.

Ben was getting desperate. Staying in the garage couldn't protect him entirely. There was a soccer game Saturday he badly wanted to play in, and besides, he had run out of both raw materials and scientific know-how for his solar project.

The garage had become more of a prison than a refuge. I tried to tell him that having other kids know wasn't as bad as he thought, but he said it was because I was a girl and people were never as hard on girls as they were on boys. Actually, I wasn't getting much teasing, not because I'm a girl, but because some of the other mothers had joined the strike, so there were other kids in the same boat. The only really serious effect was that the guys were acting nervous around the girls, as if we were tainted with the same craziness as our mothers just because we were female. (It wasn't all that hard on me, because the boys I cared about—like John Bertoni—hadn't paid any attention to me *before* the strike.) Mostly, everyone at school tried to avoid talking about it, as if ignoring the whole mess might make it go away—or at least keep it from getting worse.

Marcia was expecting to get a good grade and lots of extra credit for her report and Rick had been invited to spend as much time as he wanted at Joey's house eating cookies. In terms of our relationship with the rest of the world, we were at least surviving. Except for Dad.

I haven't fairly introduced Dad yet. Michael Richard Skinner is sort of a cross between Ward Cleaver (if you get "Leave It to Beaver" reruns where you are, you'll know him) and Clint Eastwood. He doesn't look like either of them, being under six feet tall and slightly overweight, with dark hair that is getting a little gray at the sides and a little thin on top. It's just that he has Ward Cleaver's tendency to talk reasonably to his children about important issues (Ben calls this lecturing) and Clint Eastwood's determination to get what he wants. Like Ben, he hates to be embarrassed in public. So Dad was actually in worse shape than anybody else, because he was being embarrassed on all sides, and couldn't go hide out in the garage. It didn't take much imagination to guess what it must have been like for him at work after the newspaper article.

That evening Dad was being more Clint Eastwood than Ward Cleaver. He refused to discuss the Ninety-five Theses with anybody. He would only say that Mom was in the wrong and that accepting her conditions would be the same as saying she was right. Her strike, he said, was a hostile act—a declaration of war. When he said that, he looked angry, but a little hurt, too—the way George Washington must have looked when he found out about Benedict Arnold. The thing was, even Clint Eastwood could hardly ignore the fact that dinner had been a disaster. Besides that, our dressers and closets were almost empty and we all needed clothes for the next day. "We'll all have to pitch in," Dad said.

Ben groaned loudly. Dad ignored him. Czar Nicholas jumped onto the table and began licking at the gravy in the bottom of the turkey roll's foil pan. Dad did not ignore this. "Why can't this animal join the strike, too?" he asked, shoving him to the floor. Dad has never been a cat person. Buffy has always been *his* pet. This George Washington had two Benedict Arnolds.

"Jenny, you will be in charge of getting some laundry done tonight. Choose one person to help you. The other two will clean up the kitchen." Dad looked at the table. "I'll have to go back to the store."

Just as I was about to choose Marcia as my helper (she's the neat, practical one—I'm no fool!) Marcia stood up. "I'll go with you, Dad," she said. "You can't just go to 7-Eleven

again. They don't have everything we need." Anyone who
had bought a frozen turkey roll in the first place needed
practical Marcia more than I did, I realized.

"That's okay, I can do the laundry alone, if everybody
brings down their dirty clothes."

It was a mistake. Half an hour later, as the darkness outside kept reminding me that I should be doing homework
or watching TV, I was standing in the shadowy basement
at the foot of an Everest of dirty clothes, reading the directions on the detergent box. It was already eight o'clock and
it was clear that there were far too many clothes to fit into
one washer load. I'd seen enough commercials to know some
things about doing laundry. I knew, for instance, that you're
not supposed to use hot water on colors. And that you're
supposed to separate white clothes from colored ones. I could
read the dials on the washer and dryer well enough to know
that you're supposed to use different cycles for different
kinds of fabrics. But the more I looked at that pile of clothes,
the more discouraged I got.

If I did whites, everybody would have clean underwear,
some would have socks, and Dad would have one shirt. If I
did darks, everybody would have jeans, Dad would have
slacks and socks, two people would have tee-shirts. Neither
load would clothe anyone completely. Then there were
whole bunches of clothes that weren't white and weren't
dark. They were sort of in the middle in terms of color, but
different from each other in terms of fabric. For instance,
did my apricot jeans, Rick's gray sweat shirt, all of Dad's
pastel shirts, Ben's corduroy pants, and my bras belong in
one wash? What temperature? What wash time? Were they
delicate (my bras) or heavy soil (Rick's sweat shirt), cotton
(my jeans), or permanent press (Dad's shirts)? I imagined

myself running a cycle for everything. I would still be sitting in the basement as the sun came up. With no homework done, I'd be in trouble all day. Wouldn't it be better to have my work done and show up in the same old clothes again? But then I imagined myself going into a classroom and taking my seat, only to have all the other kids (led by John Bertoni) get up and move to the back of the room, like in a commercial about failed deodorant.

If I ran only one load, we'd either have to wear dirty underwear under clean clothes, or dirty clothes over clean underwear. It was impossible! Finally, I decided to choose one outfit for every person and wash them all together with medium temperature and a medium cycle, hoping for the best.

That's why we all wore clean pink underwear the next day, why my apricot jeans are splotched with orange, and Dad's cream shirt isn't cream any more. How was I to know that Rick's red shirt was brand new? Anyway, it wasn't until afterward that I found the little tag that said to wash it separately the first few times. The blue jeans were part of that single load and they didn't do any damage at all. People ought to remember that it could have been worse!

Besides, mine wasn't the only catastrophe that evening. Ben and Rick did the dishes, all right. I heard them clunking around and yelling at each other for nearly an hour. Afterwards, they went to bed. When I got up to the kitchen, after folding the last of the pink clothes, I was greeted by the sight of bubbles pouring out over the top and around the sides of the dishwasher door. Froth was sliding down the harvest gold front and dripping onto the floor, where a ridge of white was beginning to move toward the refrigerator. Czar Nicholas was watching with great fascination. It wasn't hard to guess what had happened. They'd used regular dish-washing detergent from the bottle next to the sink instead of the automatic-dishwasher powder from the box under the sink. It suddenly dawned on me that neither Rick nor Ben had ever run the dishwasher before.

Luckily, Dad and Marcia got home just about that time, so I didn't have to clean it up by myself. Unluckily, before I had time to warn her, Marcia, her arms loaded with groceries, stepped into the froth on the floor. That was how the eggs and milk, the bread and hamburger, ended up on the floor, too. Even that could have been worse, though. Only three eggs broke, the plastic bag kept the bread from getting wet, and the hamburger was only slightly dented. But it was a long time before we had the mess cleaned up, the groceries put away, and could go to bed ourselves. I ended up not getting my homework done after all. I don't think it was an accident that Marcia kept slamming the bathroom and bed-room doors while she was getting ready for bed, but it probably didn't work. Ben and Rick both sleep pretty soundly.

DEMONSTRATIONS

It's too depressing to recount every bit of the next couple of days in detail. However, some of the high points (maybe I should say low points) might be worth mentioning. Press coverage of the strike grew to national proportions and the ranks of local women coming and going on our front lawn expanded. Representatives of the National Organization for Women and several other groups (including the ACLU, for some reason) came to talk to Mom. She was a celebrity. Phone calls from NBC, ABC, CBS, and the Donahue show failed to reach her, since Dad refused to take any calls for her on our phone. Gradually the calls for her decreased. I began to wonder whether the phone company would install a phone in a tent.

Meanwhile, calls for Dad increased astronomically. Some of his calls were from national groups as well—groups like the National Rifle Association, the Moral Majority, and the KKK. Most of them seemed to be threatening calls, accusing Dad of allowing his wife to destroy the American family. Even we recognized this as gross exaggeration. I never did figure out why the National Rifle Association got into it. Finally, Dad was driven to getting us a new, unpublished phone number. Despite our protestations that this would destroy our social lives, he insisted that we tell *no one* our new number. He was under so much strain that we decided not to point out the obvious fact that a phone for which no one knew the number was not a very useful instrument of communication. Anyway, I decided that "no one" couldn't mean Sarah, so even though we weren't on the best of terms, I gave her the number in case of emergency.

I did have a high point in there somewhere. It was when Sarah told me she couldn't come home with me after school, not because she didn't want to cross a picket line, but because she had to vacuum her house before she helped fix dinner. It seems that even though Sarah hadn't understood the true meaning of the strike, her mother had. "Rachel says she must have felt guilty all this time," Sarah told me grumpily, "for depriving us of a father. So she'd been doing all the work just the way she always had. Now she says we're not only going to be liberated, we're going to be equal, too." I couldn't give Sarah as much sympathy as she wanted, but I was glad to have my best friend back on my side.

Domestic matters in our household deteriorated steadily, with nutrition leading the way. Czar Nicholas was the only one who made out at all, because everyone kept leaving fairly decent-sized portions of their meals for him. The trouble was, all of Mom's cookbooks seemed to think we already knew how to cook. They were full of directions like "cream together sugar and shortening" and "lower heat and simmer until tender." If you don't know what "cream" means except some heavier form of milk, and when your stove doesn't have a lower heat called "simmer," it's hard to follow that kind of direction. To give everybody credit, we all tried, except Rick. (Dad wouldn't let him near the stove for fear he'd forget, leave it on, and burn the house down.)

First Dad and Ben tried, then Marcia and I tried, and then we went to frozen foods again. That's when we learned that a frozen entree that claims to serve four is only a decent size for Dad, with maybe a bite or two left over. Meanwhile, Dad was getting more and more touchy about money. Convenience foods are expensive.

The next major event happened on Saturday. Freed from their regular routines at jobs or whatever, all the nuts in town showed up outside our house on Saturday morning. When I got home from spending the night at Sarah's, they were there. On one side of the yard was a group of women carrying placards denouncing Mom and her group. These women were dressed like Suzie Homemaker dolls, in dresses. And despite their apparent intention of standing, or walking, around all day, they were all wearing high heels. Some of them had bouffant hair styles that must have been preserved since the early 60's. They were like a living museum. The signs they were carrying said things like "Save the Family" and "Motherhood is Holy!" There was even one that said "Abortion is Murder!" Probably it was left over from some other demonstration, and the woman hadn't had time to make a new one. A couple of the women had strollers with them. I wondered how the little kids strapped into their strollers felt about being there. It looked like a pretty boring way to spend a Saturday, even for a baby.

On the other side of the yard was another group, also carrying placards. This group was mixed, though—some men and some women. Actually, the men outnumbered the women. They were all pretty young, and every one, I kid you not, *every one*, was wearing blue jeans and running shoes. These people were not about to hurt *their* feet! There was a good deal of long hair, on both men and women, and most of the men wore beards. Their placards said things like "Parent-hood, an Equal Opportunity Employment" and "Fathers Can Parent Too." Rick, who came out only briefly during a commercial in "Bugs Bunny/Road Runner," pointed out that one guy in that group was carrying a sign that also said "Save the Family." Rick thought the two groups ought to get to-gether so half of them could go home. He didn't seem to grasp the whole picture.

Some of the people in the second group also had kids with them, but there wasn't a stroller in sight. These kids were in backpacks except for a tiny baby whose hair was just visible at the top of one of those little snuggly things that one guy was wearing on his chest. What I noticed was an absence on both sides of older kids. It looked as if both Parenthood and Motherhood were easier to flaunt when kids were still little enough to tie down and take with you.

Occasionally, members of these two groups shouted some-thing at each other, but mostly the women in the Suzie Homemaker bunch shouted at Mom and her crew. Our yard had changed in appearance radically by this time. Another tent had gone up next to ours (Ben said it was probably the latrine tent) and there were a couple of card tables and folding chairs. Women were sitting at those tables with papers and pens, doing some kind of work. The picket line was now quite clearly a path, with not a blade of grass left along it at all, and it wasn't just Mom walking it any more—other women were taking turns. The Pennsylvania map sign had been joined by others proclaiming the name of the group: Wives and Mothers Against Discrimination, or Wives/MAD. The thing about Mom's group was that there wasn't a child in sight, little or big. These women were not flaunting their motherhood, they were rejecting it.

Dad slept late that day. At least he stayed in his room late that day. I doubt that he'd been sleeping with all that ruckus going on outside. When he finally did come downstairs, he certainly didn't look rested. I was making some brownies from a mix, so I was in the kitchen when he came down looking rumpled and gloomy. He got himself a cup of instant coffee, grumbling incoherently the whole time, and rummaged in the refrigerator for some breakfast. He settled for an English muffin everyone else had rejected. It was the one that got hard when somebody left the bag open, but it was also the last one. He slathered it with peanut butter (fast becoming our main source of protein), moved the dirty cereal bowls and plates that were on the table, and sat down.

Before he had time to munch his way through his breakfast, there was a knock at the door. When I opened it, Mr. Anderson was there, holding Amy by the hand and looking almost as bad as Dad. He barged right past me, dragging Amy with him, and stood in front of the table. "All right, Mike, what are you going to do about this?"

Dad looked up at him, took a sip of his coffee and shrugged his shoulders. "About what, Harry?" Even under stress, Dad does okay when he's had some coffee.

"You know damned well what! This strike of Eleanor's. This craziness!"

Dad looked at Amy and then at me. I could see what was coming, but couldn't figure out how to stop it. I'd never much cared for Amy Anderson, but it was clear that I was going to have to spend part of my Saturday in her company anyway. I chalked up another mental mark against Mom. "Jenny," Dad said, in his most reasonable Ward Cleaver voice, "why don't you take Amy someplace and entertain her

for a while so her father and I can talk?" Before I could
think of a single excuse, Mr. Anderson had transferred his
daughter's sticky little hand to mine, and that was that. Amy
stuck the thumb of her other hand into her mouth and
followed me into the family room, where Rick was still
watching television. I don't know what other three year olds
do with their lives, but Amy Anderson doesn't seem to do
anything. I don't think she even talks. I hoped she at least
liked cartoons. As we left the kitchen, I heard Mr. Anderson
say something about "contagious diseases," and I remembered seeing Mrs. Anderson at one of the card tables on the
front lawn that morning. I suspected Mr. Anderson didn't
know much more about what to do with Amy than I did.

I tried to leave Amy with Rick and Fat Albert so I could
go back and find out what was going on in the kitchen, but
every time I got out of her sight, Amy would take her thumb
out of her mouth long enough to shriek. Whatever else she
did, Amy shrieked impressively. So the whole time Dad and
Mr. Anderson were talking in the kitchen, I was stuck watching Fat Albert warn America's little kids about the dangers
of smoking pot.

Rick was with us, of course. Marcia was outside, going
from group to group talking to everyone and taking notes
for her report. Ben had eaten some cereal, put on a pair of
sunglasses (he'd taken to wearing them every time he left
the house), and gone off on his bike. He'd gone back to
school, so he'd decided not to miss his soccer game after all.
Without Mom to drive him, though, he had to leave an hour
early to get there on time.

None of us were there, then, when Dad and Mr. Anderson
began making plans to fight back. Their new army hadn't
gotten very far when the sirens started.

CIVIL DISORDER
AND CHAOS

It was just bad luck that Marcia happened to be with the "Motherhood is Holy" crowd when the fighting broke out, because until moments before, she had been inside one of the tents, taking notes about the new members of Wives/ MAD. She had just come out and was interviewing one of the women with bouffant hair, when the atmosphere, which had been the kind of minor hostility you associate with football games, changed suddenly. It all happened so fast that she couldn't be sure exactly how it started or who struck the first blow, but she did know it had to do with the two people who were both carrying signs that said "Save the Family." First, they'd gotten into a shouting match about how to accomplish that goal, and then somebody apparently hit somebody else with a sign. After that, people started throwing things at each other—mostly food from the lunches everybody had brought along—and then the two groups came together. There was a lot of shoving and name calling and even some hair pulling, but Marcia didn't think anybody was really getting hurt. She was trying to keep out of the way of the fight, but still stay close enough to see and record it for her report, when the police arrived and began loading people into patrol cars. She says they must have been waiting for something like that to happen, because they got there so fast. However they got there, Marcia was one of the first people who got taken away.

The thing is, none of us noticed that at the time. After the excitement died down, we went back inside, Dad grumbling that not a single member of Wives/MAD had been arrested. He turned on the Penn State game, which both he and Mr. Anderson wanted to watch, and I found myself still in charge of Amy. I took her to the kitchen to help me finish the brownies. Her help consisted mainly of sticking her fingers into the batter and nearly chopping off her tongue trying to lick the eggbeater.

When the phone call came to inform Dad that his younger daughter was being held at Juvenile Hall, and when he had finally stopped sputtering and threatening lawsuits, I offered to go along to spring Marcia. I thought we ought to take Amy Anderson and leave her there with the rest of the delinquents, but I gladly turned her over to her father so I could go with Dad.

Viewed from the outside, Juvenile Hall is a building so depressing it looks as if perfectly ordinary kids would turn into delinquents just from staying there overnight. It was once a house, but now it's so rundown it looks more like a Jaycees Halloween fund-raising project. Inside, it's even worse. There is this long, dark hall with dirty walls that are lined with uncomfortable-looking wooden benches. There are holes in the plaster ceiling and dark, scarred doors leading off the hall, all closed. Bare wooden stairs with a broken banister lead up into shadowy regions above. From upstairs, when we got inside, came great thumps and shouting. I wondered if people were being tortured up there. Nobody but Marcia, I thought, could be there without falling apart. But there she was, sitting on one of those awful benches, her steno pad on her lap, cheerfully talking to a large woman in a dark uniform who was sitting behind a battered desk not far inside the front door.

As soon as she saw Dad, the woman stood up—and up (she looked about six and a half feet tall) and stretched out a very large hand. "Mr. Skinner?" she asked. Dad nodded, but didn't shake hands. I thought he might have been afraid of broken bones. "I'm sorry about this mix-up," the woman said.

"Mix-up? Mix-up?" Dad asked. He was more Clint Eastwood than I'd ever seen him. "I would say it was more serious than a mix-up when the police snatch a ten-year-old child off her own front lawn and throw her in jail!"

"It was a mistake," the woman said. "The officers didn't know until they had taken her to the station that the child's mother was not with her. She was taken away from the police station as soon as possible. She was certainly not 'thrown in jail,' as you put it."

Dad looked around and shuddered. "I'm sure the children who are brought here are grateful for this homelike environment!"

Marcia stood up. "It's okay, Dad." She put out her hand to the woman. "Thank you, Ms. Wyznicki, for taking the time to talk to me. This has been just about the most interesting afternoon of my whole life." She grinned at Dad. "Don't be mad! I bet I'll never have to do another thing for social studies as long as I live. This is going to be one terrific report."

Dad fumed all the way home, while Marcia told us about the police station, where they didn't fingerprint her, to her great disappointment. Her other disappointment had been that they hadn't put handcuffs on her for the trip to Juvenile Hall. "That would've been great!" she said. "They did put handcuffs on the guy who went with me. He was on some kind of drug and kept trying to slug the cops who brought him in, so they had to handcuff him before they could get him into the car."

When Dad had regained control of the car—which he'd almost driven off the road—he announced that he would write the chief of police, the mayor, and probably the governor.

He wasn't willing to take the view that Marcia had spent an educational afternoon. For someone who doesn't like public spectacles, it had not been a good day—or a good week. While the events of that particular Saturday couldn't really be blamed directly on Mom, I still didn't think they would help change Dad's attitude about the Ninety-five Theses. And that was even before we got home to discover that the Penn State game was over, and that both Rick and Mr. Anderson had been so interested in the game that they'd forgotten about Amy, who had used the time to tear the Saturday paper (which Dad hadn't read yet) into hundreds of tiny pieces, which she had then scattered throughout the house in an apparent attempt to imitate Hansel and Gretel being led into the forest.

As Dad stood in the litter of his newspaper, Ward Cleaver was driven out once and for all. He sent Marcia to her room, in spite of her protestations that he was punishing the victim for the unfair actions of the police. Then he sent Rick to find Ben (who had come home from the soccer game his team had lost, in time to see the last of the police cars pulling away, and had disappeared into his room) with orders that the two of them find out the names of all the women who had newly joined the strike, however they could manage it. I was ordered to take Amy back to her own house and put her down for a nap. I didn't even bother to argue. So much for the rest of Saturday.

As I dragged an unwilling Amy across the yards and up to her bedroom, I couldn't decide whether I was madder at Mom, for starting this whole thing, or at Dad, for turning me into a mother substitute. I hate baby-sitting, even for money, and I'd noticed that nobody'd mentioned money in connection with this job.

It was not easy to get out of Amy's room. She shrieked every time I tried to leave her until she finally fell asleep in the middle of my fifth reading of *Tubby the Tuba* (which is barely tolerable, even once!) As I went downstairs to find something to eat or drink, I remembered Mom's use of the term "patriarchy" and thought I understood it a little better than I had the week before. But then I found an adult paperback on the coffee table and settled down on the couch with it and a Coke, and the truth is, I got too interested in the book to pursue any line of thought about our situation at all. In fact, I even forgot to resent having to stay with Amy.

Dad and Mr. Anderson spent what was left of the afternoon calling the homes of the women whose names Ben and Rick brought back. While the boys' information wasn't always completely accurate and some of the calls were therefore embarrassing, the overall result was exactly what Dad had hoped for. Husbands were overwhelmingly enthusiastic about joining a group to oppose the Wives/MAD strike. The first meeting of the new group was set for the next evening.

At some point, Ben and Mr. Anderson went out to get food, drink and charcoal (both Dad and Mr. Anderson are better at cooking on a grill than on a stove) and by the time they returned, Ben had been transformed from an almost-thirteen-year-old recluse to a Committed Soldier. He had turned all the energies he usually reserved for his projects and inventions to the task of organizing the new group. He even thought up the name: Children and Husbands Against Offensive Strikes, otherwise known as CHAOS.

Marcia, having had a trying day, had fallen asleep when she'd been sent to her room. That, and not having had lunch, probably accounts for the fact that even after being busted, even after long talks with the women of Wives/MAD for her report, she was ready to join CHAOS when Dad told us about it over dinner. Had she spent her time thinking instead of sleeping, she says, she would have felt very differently. Personally, I think that's only hindsight.

In any case, good food is probably at least as central to life as money. That evening's meal was without a doubt the best we'd had since the strike began. As we all gathered around the picnic table in the Andersons' backyard to eat grilled steaks, roasted potatoes and deli cole slaw, even Amy's wandering around the table trying to grab things from other people's plates didn't dampen our good spirits.

When we'd finished huge bowls of rocky road ice cream (the only thing Amy was willing to sit still to eat) we all felt good, ready to listen to Dad and Mr. Anderson. Their theory was that we could take the wind out of the Wives/MAD sails by showing them that we simply didn't need the services they were withholding. What we needed was to make a strong show of self-sufficiency. In fact, what we needed was to hint that far from being in trouble, we might actually be better off as we were. "We must not allow ourselves to be forced to give away what are natural rights and privileges," Mr. Anderson said.

"You children have a very important job already," Dad said. "A full-time job. That job is to get an education! You have school and you have homework, and you shouldn't be burdened down with domestic responsibilities, except for minor tasks like making beds or helping with dishes from time to time."

This seemed to me to be a very reasonable position. Who needed to stay up half the night doing laundry or cleaning the kitchen when there were twenty-five math problems and a chapter of history to do?

"My job," Dad went on, "and Harry's job, is to earn the money that puts roofs over our heads and food in our mouths. It isn't our job to cook that food."

"Mom works—" Marcia said.

"She *did* work," Dad corrected. "I'm willing to admit that the money her job brought in was very helpful. It has enabled us to live better than we could have otherwise. However—" here Dad smacked the table with his fist so hard that Amy got scared and started to cry. He had to wait until she calmed down before he could finish. "However," he repeated, when Amy stuck her thumb in her mouth again, "if I quit my job and we tried to live on your mother's salary, we couldn't even afford a roof! Besides, the fact that she's in a position to quit suddenly, as she has done, shows that her contribution isn't essential to our existence. We'll have to cut back, but we'll manage.

"Your mother's primary job," Dad continued, "is to see that the house and the family are taken care of. I don't say that she can't have another job, only that it shouldn't interfere with her primary job. I'm in charge of the work at my office, and she's in charge of the work at home. When we were married, I knew I'd have to spend my life earning a living and she knew she'd have to spend hers taking care of our home and children. My work includes a lot of things I don't like doing, but I can't stop doing them. Your school-work includes a lot of things you don't like doing." We all nodded vigorously. "But you can't stop doing those things either. We all have roles to play. It doesn't make sense for the roles to be the *same*."

"I'm going to be a sociologist," Marcia announced. "I'm not going to get married and have kids at all."

Dad looked at her in surprise. Marcia's plans for her career changed often, but everybody always thought she intended to get married, too. "Well," Dad said, frowning, "I suppose that's a choice you have a right to make."

"I'm not getting married then, either," Rick said. "Because I'm going to be a television producer."

Dad laughed. "You can be a television producer and still be a husband—and a father, too."

"Oh." Rick looked confused. To tell the truth, I was feeling a little confused myself. Something wasn't going together right. Marcia was staring off into space, and I wasn't even sure she'd heard.

Ben apparently hadn't been listening to us at all. "I think I know how CHAOS can work," he said.

Amy, probably bored by everything since the ice cream, struggled out of her father's lap and went off into the yard. Mr. Anderson began to stack the dishes while he listened to Ben.

"Each family has just about the same basic things to do while the strike goes on, right?"

Everyone nodded. "Well, it seems like a waste for each family to have to do every one of those things—the cooking and the cleaning and the laundry and the yard work. We could do it in teams. There could be a team that just mowed and raked lawns. And a team that collected grocery lists and then did all the shopping in one big trip. There could be a team that picked up laundry and took it to one of those laundromats with the great big washers—"

"What about food?" I asked. "You can't set up a community kitchen."

"Potluck suppers!" Ben answered. "Instead of each family having to make a vegetable dish and a meat dish and a salad and a dessert, each family could make just one, then we could all get together and share. We could take turns having it at different houses and if somebody's house isn't big enough, they could take the days when it's nice enough to eat outside."

"Way to go, Ben," Dad said. "Teamwork! We'll lick this thing yet!"

"What about a baby-sitting team?" Mr. Anderson asked.

"That would be harder," Ben said. "I haven't got that one figured out yet. It would be easy enough after school, but what would we do with kids like Amy while the rest of us are in school and you guys are at work?"

"Hire somebody," Dad said.

Mr. Anderson shook his head. "Not as easy as it sounds. I've been through my wife's list of sitters and they're all high school girls. The one agency that's listed in the phone book costs a fortune and they only work by the hour."

"What does your wife do when she has to go out during the day?" Marcia asked.

"I don't know. I think she just takes Amy along."

"Why don't you do that, then?" Rick asked. "Why don't

you take Amy to work with you?" We all laughed. "What's so funny?"

"You can't take a child to work," Dad explained.

"Then leave her at home."

"She's too young to stay by herself," Mr. Anderson said.

Rick shrugged. "It looks to me like you need Mrs. Anderson after all."

"We'll think of something," Dad said, hurriedly. "There are quite a few fathers with the same problem."

"Maybe you can find one who works nights," Marcia suggested. "Then he could take all the little kids during the day, and somebody else could take them at night."

Before anybody had a chance to respond to that suggestion, hysterical shrieks split the air. While we'd been talking, Amy had wandered over to the bird bath at the back of the yard and had managed to pull it over on herself. She was lying on the ground on her back, soaked with greenish water. Luckily, the bird bath was plastic and not cement. It would be hard, I thought, to find anybody *but* a mother to take care of Amy.

That ended the meeting. By the time we'd cleaned up, it was dark, and we went home. I looked out the dining room window at the glow coming from the tents on the front lawn, and wondered if Mom knew about Marcia and the police. For a minute, I wanted to go out and tell her, partly because she'd probably want to know, and partly because I wanted to tell somebody about the whole day, and Sarah had gone to her grandmother's for the rest of the weekend. But we were in a combat situation, Dad had said, and Mom was the enemy. It was weird, I thought, that I'd forgotten that, even for a moment. Weird.

At eleven, when the news came on, the first local story was about the "riot" on our front lawn. Marcia pointed to an elbow sticking out from behind a burly cop who was herding somebody toward a patrol car, but the elbow was gone before anybody could be sure it was actually hers. She was excited about her first appearance on television, but the excitement was decidedly diminished by the fact that so little of her actually showed. Rick was so jealous that she'd gotten to ride in a police car with the siren on that he insisted it wasn't her elbow anyway. Then he announced that he intended to move out to the tent with Mom so he'd be sure to be on hand if another riot ever happened. Dad sent him to bed.

The weather forecast promised another Indian summer day, due to a stationary high someplace, so Dad decided we would have the first potluck supper at our house the next evening, and follow it with the first meeting of CHAOS. After the sports news, he said, we would make plans for tomorrow.

MAKING PLANS

I think I should explain that this next fairly gross part is included only so you can see the conditions under which we were working that night. It helps to explain why reasonably intelligent people could forget so many important details.

During the sports section of the news Dad found out that the Penn State game had been one of the most exciting college games in recent history. The Nittany Lions had won with an interception and a sixty-yard run for a touchdown in the last fifteen seconds. "What a game!" the announcer said. When he repeated it, Dad shut off the television abruptly. He told Ben to get some paper and bring it to the kitchen, where we could plan the first potluck supper. When we saw that it would take a half an hour or so to unearth the actual surface of the kitchen table, we adjourned to the dining room, where the table was dusty but bare.

We had barely sat down when Dad began to sniff and make faces. "What is that? Where is that terrible smell coming from?"

The rest of us began to sniff then, too. It wasn't a garbage smell, as might have been expected since the dining room is right next to the kitchen. It was worse. Much worse. There are some odors in the world that are easy to recognize, like onion or lemon or freshly baked bread. Or skunk. But as far as I'm concerned, the worst is cat pee. And the dining room absolutely reeked of cat pee. The more we sniffed, though, the worse it seemed to get. There was another odor too. It wasn't only cat *pee*.

Marcia found the source of both smells—directly under the table on the rug. Large amounts of both.

"Call the SPCA!" Dad yelled. Luckily, Czar Nicholas was nowhere to be seen. I was pretty sure he was smart enough to be hidden safely under Mom and Dad's bed, where nobody could reach him. And luckily, the SPCA is not open at 11:25 on Saturday night.

Marcia, having been the one to find the mess, found herself also having to clean it up. Generously, I brought paper towels. Dad stormed into the kitchen, grabbed a can of beer out of the refrigerator and refused to come into the dining room again until it was taken care of. Ben went upstairs— supposedly to get a pencil, since the pencil he'd brought had managed to get broken. It seemed a little too convenient an excuse. I'd read somewhere that the only possible antidote to cat pee is vinegar, so I got the gallon jug of cider vinegar from the kitchen and poured some on the rug. After that, the room smelled only a little like cat pee and a lot like salad.

"I found out why he did it," Marcia said when she returned from the downstairs bathroom where she'd disposed of the paper towels. "Nobody had cleaned the litter box. You should see it." She made a face. "Worse, you should smell it! No wonder he didn't want to go there." She looked at us accusingly. "Hasn't anybody used that bathroom lately? Couldn't anybody have noticed and cleaned the litter box?"

Nobody answered. We'd all used the bathroom. I guess it

just didn't occur to anyone to actually do anything about the litter box. None of us had before.

"Assuming we can survive the atmosphere in this room," Dad said, taking the legal pad from Ben, "we'd better get this potluck thing organized. It's late!"

"Won't it be sort of hard to have it here?" Marcia asked, "with all the women right around the house in the front yard?"

"If your mother can appropriate the front lawn, I guess I should be able to do what I want with the back."

Dad put Ben in charge of getting plenty of paper plates and cups and napkins. Marcia and I were to call all the fathers and explain about bringing one large food dish to share with everyone. Ben suggested we should get press coverage, since Wives/MAD had been getting so much attention, and Dad agreed to call the newspaper and TV people. By the time we were done, we were all pretty tired, but we were actually looking forward to the next evening. No one was bothered by the ominous sound of "The First CHAOS Potluck Supper."

SUNDAY, OCTOBER 9

The big day dawned, as had the previous seven days, with a clean, crisp blue sky and a bright autumn sun. Dad usually sleeps until noon on Sunday, getting up only in time for brunch and to read the Sunday paper before the football games. But this Sunday he was up by nine o'clock, positively bustling around. He'd already been up long enough to have a cup of instant coffee when he banged on our doors, shouting, "Rise and shine!" like a demented camp counselor. "Everybody up! Out of bed, there's work to be done! Up, up, up!"

Ordinarily, I don't mind getting up on weekends. But to be wakened by somebody shouting about work is unfair! I pulled the covers over my head and tried to pretend I hadn't heard the racket he was making. But then Dad sent Rick, who's always up early, to rout us out. He did it by first jumping onto Marcia's bed and tickling her and then, before she could untangle her covers enough to hit him, scooting over to pull the blankets off my bed. "Come on," he said, as he headed for the door again. "Dad wants everybody down in five minutes. Dressed!"

Rick, I'd noticed, was wearing the red shirt that had been responsible for the pink laundry, and the same old jeans.

Now that I thought about it, I couldn't remember seeing him in anything else since then—so he must have been wearing the same clothes since Thursday. I didn't even know if he'd bothered with pajamas for sleeping. I climbed reluctantly out of bed and went to check my own clothing situation. I'd already dragged out blouses that had been in the back of the closet so long the shoulders were dusty. By now there was nothing left but a pair of too-short jeans and a Budweiser tee-shirt I'd bought in extra large to wear as a night shirt, and which had shrunk up but not in. It was now very wide, but just barely long enough to cover my belt. As for underwear, I'd hoped for the last two days that I wouldn't get hit by a car, because it would have been very embarrassing to have the hospital staff see the rags I'd had to resurrect.

When we got to the kitchen, it was clear that we were all in the same condition. Marcia had on some hand-me-downs that were still too big for her, Ben had on jeans that barely reached his ankles and had to be held together at the waist by an elastic belt because he couldn't keep them snapped. Dad was wearing the clothes he usually reserved for painting ceilings, all speckled with tiny spots of white.

"The first order of business is laundry," Dad observed, looking over his motley and yawning work crew. "Jenny, you and Marcia can take care of that. I'll do your phoning for you." He looked at Rick. "Did you put those clothes on fresh this morning?"

I laughed. "Fresh" was hardly the word.

When Rick shook his head, Dad sent him up to change so we could wash those clothes. I wasn't altogether sure washing would help them at this point. "Meantime," Dad turned to Ben, "how about getting started with the kitchen? The table needs to be cleared and the dishes washed."

"Can't we have breakfast first?" Ben asked.

"Okay. Right. Breakfast." Dad looked around at the littered and sticky counter tops. "What'll we have?"

"How about the usual?" Marcia suggested. "It's Sunday."

The usual was Eggs Benedict, Mom's specialty. Sometimes she made crepes, or popovers, or blueberry coffee cake, but everybody liked Eggs Benedict best. Dad frowned. "Too fattening," he said. "How about some nice, crisp Cheerios?" We shook our heads. "Instant oatmeal?" Same response. "Okay." He straightened his back and rubbed his hands together. "Okay, if it's Eggs Benedict you want, it's Eggs Benedict you'll get." He looked at me. "You want to help?"

"No, thanks, I've got that laundry to do, remember? How about gathering up whatever dirty clothes are upstairs?" I said to Marcia. "I'll go down and get started with the sorting."

She started out of the kitchen and collided with Rick, who appeared suddenly, wearing a pair of Superman pajamas. "Look what I found!" he said. "Under the sheets in my drawer. I didn't even know I had them!"

"Where'd you leave the other things?" Marcia asked.

"I don't remember," he said cheerfully. "In my room, I guess."

"Marcia!" Dad called, as she left, muttering darkly. "Don't bother with my shirts. I'm taking them to the cleaners." He took down a cookbook and began scanning the table of contents. "They iron them," he told me, "even though they're permanent press."

I headed for the basement. If he thought permanent press

clothes should be ironed, he'd better keep on taking things to the cleaners!

This time, as I stood facing the washer and dryer, I noticed that there were little pockets at the back of each holding pamphlets called "Laundry Guides." From the amount of lint and dust on them, I was sure Mom hadn't ever used them. But I wasn't Mom, and I didn't have some mystical communion with household appliances. This time, I would read the manufacturer's instructions and do it right. When Marcia brought the clothes down, I sent her back up to help in the kitchen where her neatness was needed. With the Laundry Guides, I figured this was a one-person job.

First, I threw in the white clothes, then put the detergent and bleach in their respective places. Then I punched up hot/hot for wash and rinse, pulled out the knob and listened to the reassuring sound of the washer filling. This time, I felt in control.

Since I didn't smell the Canadian bacon part of the Eggs Benedict yet, I went ahead and sorted the rest of the clothes according to the directions. It took a long time, thanks to the fact that everybody in the family except Marcia seemed to take clothes off inside out, and I had to put them back right side out again. And check the pockets. (I took the quarter and two dimes I found in Ben's jeans—fair's fair.) Rick's clothes took the longest, because I had to spray stain stuff on every single shirt and on the knees of all his pants. But this was going to be a perfectly-done laundry. We were going to prove we could be self-sufficient.

When all the clothes had been sorted into neat piles, pre-treated and pocket-checked, I went up to see if breakfast was ready. Progress had been made. The table had been unearthed, a green trash bag was in the middle of the floor, bulging with the remains of recent meals and a week's worth of newspapers (Dad had refused to be bothered with recycling them in spite of Marcia's admonitions). Marcia was at the sink, washing the dishes that couldn't be put in the dishwasher. On closer inspection, I saw that she was actually engaged in a subtle attack on Rick, who was drying. Every time he would reach for a dish, Marcia would squirt the sprayer and try to get his hand.

"You're scalding me!" he yelled, finally. "And anyway, it isn't my fault. I didn't ask to dry. Dad assigned me!"

"Because you said you were afraid you might drop something and break it in the soapy water," she said, threatening to squirt him again. "You just didn't want to wash, you little creep!"

Ben was scrubbing at something on the top of the stove with grim determination. "Shut up, you two," he said. "Let's just get done. And the next time somebody lets cheese melt on a burner, that person is the one who has to clean it off!"

"Where's Dad?" I asked. "And where's the Eggs Benedict?"

"He went to get doughnuts," Rick said. "We don't have the right kind of eggs."

Marcia sprayed Rick one last time and turned off the water. "The real reason is that he read the directions for making hollandaise sauce. Right after that he said we had the wrong size eggs. Then he went to get doughnuts. Some self-sufficiency—doughnuts!"

"It's okay with me," Rick said. "I'm starved." He dropped his towel and flung himself on the floor, writhing in spectacular agony. "I'm turning into a skeleton. I haven't had any lunch since last Tuesday!"

"Why not?" Marcia asked. "I bought peanut butter and jelly and apples, and there are still some Granola bars."

Rick sat up. "You mean I was supposed to make my own?"

"Well, what did you think?"

"You made both our lunches the first day."

"Well, sure. We had to split what little food there was. Do you really mean that you haven't had lunch since then?"

Rick shook his head. He'd been acting, but now real tears began to slide down his cheeks. "Not once. Joey's mom put in a cupcake for me on Friday. I had that."

"Jeez," Marcia said. "You could have told somebody!"

"I kept forgetting."

Dad arrived with the doughnuts then, so we all sat down and ate Bavarian creams. And to think Dad had said Eggs Benedict would be fattening! Cupcakes and doughnuts. I wondered how long it takes to get scurvy.

The rest of the day was devoted to the house and yard. Ben mowed the grass. Rick dusted. At least, that's what he was assigned to do. Actually, he kept forgetting what he was doing and played Superman, making a cape of his dust rag and jumping off the furniture. When he did remember what he was doing—usually when Dad happened to be around— he sort of flicked the rag around the edges of things. Marcia was assigned to clean the bathrooms, an assignment she protested mightily. Dad ignored her protestations. When he assigned me to vacuum, I didn't even bother to point out that I still had laundry to do. Dad was now Clint Eastwood playing General Patton and wasn't discussing anything.

General Patton's entire contribution to the day was to phone the men and tell them about the potluck supper. As I vacuumed, I thought of Mom outside where there were no rugs to be swept or shelves to be dusted, surrounded by her growing army of friends, playing general for her side. And Dad, the phone at his ear, playing general for his side. While the four of us worked. Kids always come out at the bottom, it seemed to me. Kids never get to be generals.

THE FIRST (AND ONLY) CHAOS POTLUCK SUPPER

When Dad called us together in the kitchen late that afternoon, we were no longer a fresh and hearty group of soldiers, if ever we had been. We were tired, hungry and grumpy. But the laundry was done, folded and safely put in drawers or closets, the lawn was mowed and raked, and the house looked good. Not perfect, maybe, but neat and fairly clean. Marcia had had the idea of gathering up all the junk lying around the house and putting it into boxes labeled with the owners' names. These boxes had all been taken upstairs, and while nobody had put the contents away, at least the boxes themselves were out of sight and the stuff wasn't all over the house any more. Ben had gone on his bike to get paper plates and napkins and cups, and they were neatly stacked on the kitchen table. In fact, they were the only things on the table for a change. It was time to get ready for the supper itself.

"I want it done right!" Dad warned. "I've got a reporter and a photographer coming from the paper, and a couple of guys from TV may be here. This is our chance to show everyone that we're getting along just fine."

I thought about Rick with no lunches all week, about having to spend a whole day cleaning, about Marcia at Juvenile Hall, and decided that a little stretching of the truth could be justified if it put an end to the strike. Still, there's no way I would have called what we were doing "getting along just fine."

Dad and Mr. Anderson brought the Andersons' picnic table over from their yard and we put a plastic tablecloth on it, then set out the paper plates and cups. We filled an old copper wash kettle with ice to keep the drinks people brought cold, and put fresh charcoal in the grill. "What're we having?" Rick asked.

"Whatever people bring," Dad said.

"I hope it's steaks again."

"Don't get your hopes up," Dad warned. He looked around the yard. "Shouldn't we have chairs?" he asked.

It was a little late to think of chairs, since Mom had the folding chairs and the picnic benches around in front. Ben brought out our kitchen chairs and Mr. Anderson brought over two yard lounges. I hoped people wouldn't expect to sit at a table to eat.

Marcia made a centerpiece for the table of some mums from the garden, and Mr. Anderson brought a huge bowl of potato chips—his contribution to the meal. I hoped other people would bring something a little more nutritious, and wondered if Dad had made any suggestions. Luckily, Amy was taking a nap, so we didn't have to worry about having the centerpiece knocked over or the tablecloth pulled off.

When we had done everything we could, we changed our clothes, and by five-thirty, when the reporter and the photographer from the paper arrived, we were ready. Or we thought we were.

We began to suspect we'd forgotten a few things when the first group arrived. It consisted of two harried-looking men and four very small children. The oldest must have been about six. "How many kids will there be?" Marcia whispered. I only shrugged. We hadn't thought to ask. Each of the men was carrying a covered pot, which they brought over to the picnic table.

"By some coincidence, we both heated up baked beans," one of them said. "I hope there'll be plenty of bean lovers."

"I hope there'll be plenty of baby-sitters," Ben hissed, as another man came up the drive, holding a madly squirming toddler under one arm and trying to balance a pan in the other. Behind him trailed a boy who looked about Amy's age.

As I put that pan next to the other two, I saw that it, too, contained beans. In fact, it wasn't until the fifth pot of baked beans had joined the rest on the table that the menu of this testament to masculine independence took on any variety at all. Mr. Secrist's high-school-age daughters had made potato salad and then gone to a movie, he explained, as he handed me the bowl. "They must have known what it was going to be like," Ben whispered. "What movies are playing?"

"Loyalty!" I reminded him. "When the going gets tough . . . ."

"The tough get going. That's exactly what I had in mind."

As more men arrived, the number of small children continued to grow. It was clear that anyone old enough to stay home alone had stayed. A couple of Rick's friends were there, and Rick had quickly joined them for some kind of very loud chasing game. But they were the oldest kids except for us. There were children crawling under the hedge, children trying to climb onto the picnic table, children pushing each other, and children trying to drag their fathers away from the other fathers they were talking to. Our back-yard looked like Romper Room. Some of the fathers had thought to bring toys, so some of the kids were playing, but others were fighting about whose toys were whose.

When one little boy asked me what he could have to eat, I noticed that we'd forgotten about silverware. I gave him some potato chips and sent Ben in to get silver from the kitchen. "We don't need knives," Ben observed, plunking forks and spoons onto the table, "unless somebody comes along with some meat!" The wash kettle now contained a gallon jug of wine and plenty of beer, but not much else. I doubted the four cans of soda would satisfy all those little kids. We'd have to send someone for milk.

I had just noticed that the air was getting chilly and clouds were beginning to gather, when Marcia came over to the table, leading a small boy and a small girl. "What'll I do now? They both have to go potty."

Ben, who'd been trying to take a toy out of the hand of a little girl who was intent on beating another little girl over the head with it, came over immediately. "I'll take the boy!" he said, and hurried into the house. A few minutes later, the boy wandered out alone. Ben wasn't seen again.

"Some loyal and devoted soldier," Marcia observed. "This whole potluck supper was *his* idea!"

Dad, a beer in one hand, was making the rounds, talking to the men, introducing them to each other and to the newspaper reporter. In between, he managed to start the charcoal, so from then on I had to spend most of my time keeping the kids away from the hot grill. When Amy Anderson arrived, it didn't even make any difference. She was just one more little body. I didn't count, but probably there were no more than ten or twelve kids. It *seemed* like a hundred.

At last, somebody arrived with two packs of hot dogs and it looked as if something resembling a meal might actually be taking shape. As I was putting the hot dogs on the grill, the sound level dropped noticeably. Marcia, who had gone in to get ketchup and mustard, came back out and asked where all the kids had gone. I looked around. Sure enough, the children had disappeared, except for a boy of about five who was totally absorbed in trying to get up Ben's climbing rope into the maple tree. I called Rick over to see if he knew where everybody had gone, and he said one of them had gone around the front, and the rest of them had followed. "Of course," Marcia said. "Their mothers are there." It was a great relief to have the problem of all those kids taken off our hands.

The photographer was busy trying to gather the men into groups for pictures. He'd persuaded Dad to put on his barbecue apron, and I got moved away from the grill so he could take a picture of Dad tending the hot dogs while some of the other men stood around looking hungry, or committed, or united—whatever he was after. The fathers who weren't being grouped for that picture were clustered together, drinking their beer or wine and talking. The photographer had assured them that he wanted to get pictures of all of them, so they were all staying close by.

It was during this picture-taking session that the children returned. But not alone. Around the side of the house came the women of Wives/MAD, carrying or leading the children who had disappeared from the backyard. Some of the kids were crying as they clung to their mothers' necks, including Amy Anderson, naturally. Some of the men looked that way for a moment, and then resumed their conversations. The photographer went on trying to arrange the group by the charcoal grill to his satisfaction. But then the mothers put the children down, let go of their hands, kissed them or patted them on the head, and started back around the house again. This action was greeted by a nearly unanimous chorus of shrieks and tears. As the mothers headed resolutely for the front yard, the crying children ran after them. They clung to their legs. They demanded to be picked up. More kissing and head patting. Reassuring words. Then another attempt to leave. The hysteria got worse. Most of the men were looking that way by then, but that's all they were doing—looking. None of them made a move in the direction of their screaming sons and daughters.

The photographer, who knew a good shot when he saw it, had abandoned the group at the grill and was busy catching the whole scene on film. *Click,* went his camera, and *click, click, click.* The men, their drinks in their hands, continued to watch, as if they were paralyzed. Or as if they didn't really hear or understand what was going on. Still the mothers tried to get away and still the children cried and clung and ran after them. I think it was right then, while the guy with the camera kept muttering "great" and "fantastic" and "incredible" as he snapped away, that I began to think about everything in a new way. It was as if I'd been looking at the world through a lens that was one color and suddenly a lens of another color had been put in its place. Everything was the same, but everything was different.

Marcia was way ahead of me. "Come on," she said, and headed for the nearest group of kids. I followed her and together we rounded up screaming children and began to herd them back toward their fathers. In the process, I got kicked a couple of times and bitten once, and several kids managed to wriggle away from me, but finally we got a few of them away, then a few more. The mothers didn't say anything, they just gave us thankful looks and scooted out of sight around the house. We didn't know which kids belonged to which men, so we were just trying to get them headed back in the right general direction, when the men finally took the hint and came, reluctantly it seemed to me, to get them.

After that, the evening went completely downhill. The kids didn't care any more about food or toys or each other. They just wanted to get back around the house to where their mothers were. The fathers had to spend most of their time heading them off. Some of the older ones were bribed successfully with soda and hot dogs, but most of the littlest ones just had to be held. It was Amy who put the cap on the whole event. Having decided that a hot dog was more important to her than her mother right then, she tried to get one for herself. In order to reach it, she had grabbed the edge of the grill. Even the other children who were crying stopped at the sound of Amy's ear-splitting scream. The photographer was there in time to get a picture of Mr. Anderson trying to comfort a wailing Amy, whose hand was already beginning to blister. He had gone elsewhere by the time Mrs. Anderson came tearing around the side of the house to see what had happened and announced that they would have to take her to the hospital.

After the Andersons left, the wind kicked up and blew all the paper plates and cups off the table. Marcia and I went after them and were joined by Buffy, who had come around to check out the smell of hot dogs, and thought chasing paper plates a wonderful game. She could hardly be blamed for knocking down the little boy who got between her and the plate she was after. The men were collecting their children, most of whom were crying again, when the rain began. And through it all, the photographer was busy, thoroughly recording a different chaos than he'd been sent to find. Finally, the heavy rain forced him to run for shelter.

I suspect the only ones to benefit from the CHAOS potluck supper were McDonald's and Wendy's, where everybody probably ate. Also Buffy, who got the rest of the wet hot dogs. Hardly anything had been eaten when the rains came, so we were left with enough baked beans to last the rest of our natural lives, one bowl of really dreadful potato salad, some soggy potato chips and a kettle full of melting ice, rainwater, and beer. Whoever had brought the wine must have remembered to take it back.

By the time Marcia, Rick, and I had rounded up all the paper stuff and brought the food and the chairs in out of the rain, we were soaked and freezing. Ben still hadn't shown up. When we'd changed clothes again—Rick back into his Superman pajamas—we found Dad and the newspaper reporter sitting by a crackling fire in the family room, each with a beer in his hand, deep in conversation. Marcia looked at me, I looked back at her, and we both understood something without saying a word. We fixed cheese sandwiches for the three of us, sent Rick, protesting, up to bed, and went up to our room. As sometimes happens during a war, there was about to be a realignment of allies.

REALIGNMENT

Ever since Mom and Dad decreed that Ben and I were too old to share a room, Marcia and I have shared one. Actually, "shared" isn't exactly the right word. The most you could say is that we have breathed the same air in an otherwise carefully divided and apportioned 120 square feet.

Marcia is a compulsive neatnik, a phase I can only hope she'll outgrow. If you were to visit our room for three days in a row, you'd think she sleeps on the floor, because her bed looks exactly the same from day to day. She has thirty-seven stuffed animals, each with its own precise place on the bed. When she wakes up in the morning, even before she goes to the bathroom, she makes her bed and arranges her animals. Probably, it's unhealthy. Probably, germs are being made into that bed every day that ought to be given time to get out and away.

It isn't just Marcia's bed, of course. She always hangs her clothes up. She even puts her jeans on a hanger! A couple of years ago Mom bought sock sorters (little plastic discs with teeth in them that hold socks together in the washer and dryer) and tried to train all of us to use them, so she wouldn't have to pair socks while she was folding the laundry. They didn't catch on with anyone except Marcia.

Every night Marcia takes off her socks, turns them right side out, threads them through a sock sorter, and drops them into her laundry basket. And another thing—Marcia's desk has on its top a blotter with fake leather corners, a matching pencil holder, a calendar, and a study lamp. Nothing else. Ever. It's unnatural.

I, on the other hand, have never been a neatnik, compulsive or otherwise. When Ben and I lived together, our room looked lived in and comfortable. Ben and I are both casual (Mom calls it "slovenly") so we got along just fine. Since Marcia moved in with me, I haven't changed any. On my side of the room the bed is always unmade. I've never understood why anyone would make a bed, since you just have to unmake it again when you get into it at night. There's a constantly changing assortment of items piled on it. When I go to bed at night, I put the stuff someplace else, like on my desk chair or on my bookshelves, or—usually—on my floor. I call it "my" floor because the room is so rigidly divided that there might as well be a line drawn down the rug. I'm only allowed to put things on "my" side. Marcia says the room is so schizo that in order to stay sane in it, we should put up a curtain, like the ones they use at hospitals to keep patients from seeing each other. I deserve it as much as she does. It's hard to be comfortable when half your room looks like a motel.

We've managed to survive living together only by keeping out of each other's way as much as possible. When she has a friend over, I go someplace else, and vice versa. We never do our homework at the same time there. Since I usually can't find space at my desk, I do most of my homework on the kitchen table. At least I did. After Mom's departure for the front yard, the kitchen table had gotten so bad I'd had to switch to the dining room. The thing is, Marcia and I have at best an uneasy truce.

But when we got up to our room that night, we weren't thinking about our differences. I pushed the clothes and books off my bed and plunked down on it. Marcia came over and sat on the end. It was the first time she had ever put her actual body on my bed.

"Well?" she said. "What did you think of all that?" I just shook my head. "Listen, Jenny, I've been talking to those women out there—for my report. And I've been talking to Mom, too. Listening to her, I mean. It's made me think."

"You've been fraternizing with the enemy?"

"My report is *supposed* to be objective. I can't just write our side. Jenny, you should see the chart Mom made out before she went on strike!"

"Chart?"

"Remember Dad said it was his job to work for the money and Mom's job to take care of us and the house? She says he's said that a lot before, and he thinks he shouldn't have to come home after doing *his* job and help her with hers. So for two weeks she kept track of every minute of work anybody did around here and made a big chart. She counted Dad's job and her library job and school for us, plus homework time. And she counted Ben's soccer games and practice as work and my violin and some of your reading time, and gave Rick some play time. She says he's still young enough to count play as part of his work. On the chart the work time is filled in with colors and everybody's free time is blank. You should see it! Even with his full-time job, Dad has less work time filled in than anybody—even Rick! On weekends, the rest of us have huge blank spaces, but Mom has just about as much color in her column as she has during the week. She hardly has any time of her own. That chart made me do some thinking about what's been happening since Mom left, and I've noticed some things about our family I'd never noticed before."

"Like what?"

"Like what jobs we got today when Dad put everybody to work. Who got to clean the bathrooms? Me. And you know as well as I do who makes the worst mess in there. Rick misses the toilet about half the time. It's gross!"

"But Rick and Ben both had jobs to do."

"Sure. Rick dusted. At least he was supposed to. But who cares about dusting? If it doesn't get done, who does it hurt? It's okay if he does a rotten job. But who had to do the laundry—a huge job that everybody really needs? You. And where does that job have to be done? In the basement, while Ben is outside in the gorgeous weather, cutting the grass. And you know perfectly well that whatever Dad was doing all day, he wasn't cleaning."

"He did make all those phone calls. . . ."

But Marcia was on a roll and there was no stopping her. "And the other night, if I hadn't gone along with him to buy groceries, he probably would've come back with nothing but bread and crackers and TV dinners. Afterward, who put the groceries away?"

"Well, but Dad didn't know where anything went."

"Exactly! Did you?"

"Not all of it."

"Me either, but we got it put away, didn't we? Maybe everything wasn't where Mom keeps it, but it didn't get left out on the counters. Dad's an adult. Don't you think he could have figured out what to do with the groceries as well as we could?"

Marcia was right. It wasn't hard to see that.

"You want to hear some more?" I nodded. "You know that I'm the only person in this family who really goes crazy in a mess. But do I have my own room? No. Rick and Ben do. If we're too old to share a room with the boys, why can't we have our own rooms and Rick and Ben share? They'd get along just fine. Instead, you and I spend our lives in the middle of World War Three. You don't like it any better than I do."

If Mom's going on strike had been like an earthquake, I was beginning to feel the aftershocks. *Rumble, rumble.*

"I could go on—you keep having to baby-sit for Amy. Nobody ever asks Ben to do that. And tonight, Dad didn't even notice that Ben had disappeared. Rick got to play with his friends while you and I had to try to keep all those kids from wiping each other out. *And* take care of the food. And that doesn't even mention all those fathers worrying more about getting their pictures in the paper than about their own kids. And while we cleaned up the yard—in the rain—Dad was in here building a fire!"

I found myself looking at the Middle Earth poster over my bed. At first I was just staring, not even focusing on it. But then I really noticed it, and I might have been seeing it for the first time, even though it had been right there on my wall for more than two years. Hobbits—male. Dwarves— male. Wizards—male. Orcs—male. I tried to remember the females in Tolkien's trilogy. Not many. Eowyn, Galadriel . . . .

"Entwives!" I said, as I remembered their story.

"What?"

"Entwives. In the Tolkien books." I'd forgotten for a moment that Marcia doesn't like fantasy. Usually, she doesn't even read fiction, but if she does, it's always realistic fiction.

"Entwives were the females of a species of tree-people called the Ents. For some reason, the females had all gone away, and the Ents didn't know where they were. They had left Middle Earth ages and ages before."

"How did they have any baby Ents then?"

"That was the point. Ents lived a great long time, but they were eventually going to die out because the females had gone away. The Ents seemed to blame the Entwives for sacrificing the whole species just because they didn't like the forest—for their own selfish reasons. It just connected with all this, somehow."

"I think this is called Consciousness Raising," Marcia said. "Sarah would be happy." Then she sighed. "I don't know. The way those little kids reacted tonight, I wonder if anything can really change. A mother is a mother. The fathers might not have been very comforting, but the kids didn't seem to *want* them, either."

I yawned, and then Marcia yawned. It had been a long and tiring day. As we got ready for bed, we heard Ben go by to his room. I wondered where he had been.

When we were both settled and I'd turned out the light, I lay for a while, wondering where I stood in all this. "Have you switched to Mom's side now?" I asked Marcia.

"Mmmm," said the lump of covers on her bed.

"Is that a yes?"

"*Mmmm.*" She turned over and punched her pillow, the way she does when she's settling down to sleep and doesn't want to talk. "Yes!"

As Marcia's breathing changed and I could tell she had gone to sleep, I thought about what she'd said and added some thoughts of my own, like Dad's not paying any attention to whether Rick had lunch or not, just assuming that *somebody* was taking care of it. It was almost as if he could take that kind of responsibility or not, as if making sure his kids were fed was somehow optional. What did Dad really know about our day-to-day lives? What did Mr. Anderson know about Amy? As I began to drift toward sleep, images of Dad and Mr. Anderson started to grow branches, like trees, or Ents. No more Entings, I thought. And then I slipped into a really dumb and obvious dream full of tank battles and planes strafing forests. Dumb, but scary.

The rain and wind that ended the potluck supper also put an end to Indian summer and began a major change in the fortunes of Wives/MAD. Monday brought a constant drizzle and steadily falling temperatures. Anybody would have to give Mom and the handful of women who showed up that morning credit. They stuck to their picket line, dressed in raincoats and boots. The original strike sign was nearly shot by this time, the state of Pennsylvania on the back dripped green and Harrisburg had faded away entirely.

When I left for school that morning, I was still a little unsure of my allegiance, or at least what I was going to do about it. But I did wave at Mom, and she waved back. It was the most contact we'd had in days. It also made me feel better than I had in days.

The weather was bad enough, but the article in the newspaper that night was worse. It was so bad, in fact, that I couldn't imagine Wives/MAD surviving, no matter how brave anyone was about cold and rain. By the time I'd finished reading that article, I understood why at trials they make people swear to tell the truth, the *whole* truth, and nothing but the truth. You can certainly distort a story by what you leave out.

There were three pictures with the article, all taken at the potluck supper. One small one showed Dad in his barbecue apron with the other men behind him. Another showed Mr. Anderson trying to comfort a screaming Amy. But there was another one. A very big one. It showed the mothers trying to get away from their crying kids—all those tear-streaked little faces. The caption made sure nobody would miss the point: "Striking mothers refuse to comfort tots." Grim.

Dad might as well have written the article himself, so thoroughly did it side with CHAOS. Much was made of the pathetic baked bean dinner, as if the women were at fault instead of Dad and the rest of us who didn't think to tell people what to bring. "After a hard week of working to 'bring home the bacon,'" the article said with striking originality, "the men of CHAOS found no one to cook it, much less to serve it. Instead of a weekend of much-deserved rest, a chance to fish or golf or take in the season's football offerings, these men came home to a weekend of cleaning, doing laundry and taking care of small children whose needs didn't magically disappear when their mothers walked off the job." I thought about Dad's weekend. It was true that he'd missed the Penn State game, but it certainly hadn't been a weekend of cleaning and laundry—not for him! According to the reporter, Amy's accident had been practically a matter of life and death. He explained that Mr. Anderson had had to rush her to the hospital, but nowhere did he say that *Mrs.* Anderson was the one who decided to take her there. The reader wouldn't even know Mrs. Anderson had been there at all.

The worst part was the last paragraph. "It was a scene to wrench the heart of even the staunchest libber. The crying children begged to be picked up. They tried to cling to their mothers' legs. But their mothers were on strike. So their mothers abandoned them as the first cold drops of rain began to fall."

Abandoned them! He made it sound as if they'd put them off on an ice floe in the dead of winter or something. Not a word, of course, about their fathers. Not a word about how easily their fathers could have come to get the children. There *was* one untruth in the article. The rain didn't start until later. But I didn't think anybody could base a libel case on that.

A few minutes after I finished reading the article, Sarah called. "Rachel says most of the women will probably quit after this. Do you think they will?"

I looked out the window, through the gray, rainy dusk, to where Mom was pacing with her sign. Even Buffy wasn't next to her. "It looks as if they already have."

"Cowards!" Sarah said. "I'd have stuck it out if I'd been on strike. I wouldn't let some bad press scare me off!"

I wondered. If a perfect stranger could get upset just looking at a picture of a crying kid, it must be a whole lot harder for a mother to walk away from one who's crying and calling for her. And it must be terrible to be labeled as a person who would abandon her own child––in the rain.

"Jenny? Are you still there?"

"I'm here. I was just thinking that it must be different when you have kids."

"Maybe the answer is not to have them, then," Sarah said.

"Maybe." I thought of the Entwives again. What kind of an answer was that? *Quake, quake. Rumble, rumble.* "Sarah," I said, "if you were in my place, what would you do now?"

There was a pause. I listened to little bleeps and pings on the line. Then Sarah giggled. "I'd form a fifth column."

"A what?"

"You know, like in the movies, when the Nazis would send people into the countries they were invading to fight from the inside—by blowing up factories and stuff."

"You'd blow up factories?"

"Don't be dense. I'd be a saboteur. You know, I'd pretend I was on the CHAOS side still, but I'd do stuff that would help your mom."

Dad had said it was a war. Was it a war between the sexes? If so, I wouldn't be betraying anyone. If so, Mom's side was really my side. Was I becoming a radical feminist like Sarah? Could a radical feminist still think about John Bertoni?

That night, I told Marcia what Sarah had suggested, and she jumped at the idea. "That's perfect! And I know just how to do it. Mom was telling me that the way men have been getting out of helping around the house for ages is to avoid knowing how to do anything. Then, if you ask them to do it, they make such a mess that you never ask again. Either that, or they conveniently forget to do what you've asked until you finally have to do it yourself. We could do that."

And so it was decided. The next morning, October 11, the underground would launch its own kind of battle.

MIDDLEWORD

I invented that term. It's like a foreword,
only in the middle. I don't know how
you'll react to stumbling over this on the
way to the next chapter, but it seems
important to put it in anyway. Up till
now, I was supposed to be the spokesperson
for all four of us kids. But when Ben got
to this part of the manuscript, he clipped
this note to the next chapter:

You're Fired! FROM HERE
ON, YOU AREN'T SPEAKING
FOR ME OR RICK. WE'LL
WRITE OUR OWN SIDE!
Ben

The only reason I'm not including their
side here is because there's a difference
between saying you're going to write a
book and actually writing it. So far they
haven't.

So I'm not speaking for Ben and Rick any
more. The truth is, I'm not speaking for
Marcia either. If there's one thing this
has taught me, it's that nobody can speak
for anybody else, no matter how much they
think they agree. It's like with those
newspaper reporters. The way you see
things depends on who you are and where
you're standing.

SOLIDARITY

The next morning breakfast was pretty much like all the other P.S. (post strike) breakfasts—cold cereal, milk, orange juice, and instant coffee for Dad. There were the usual morning grumbles—Dad had to stop at the cleaner to drop off shirts again and even if they did iron them, he wasn't happy about how much it cost, or the inconvenience of having to stop there on the way to work and again later to pick them up. Rick asked him for two dollars to get lunch at 7-Eleven on his way to school, and he grumbled more. "You'd better get up in time to fix something for yourself tomorrow," Dad said. "I can't give you ten dollars a week for lunches."

When Dad and Rick and Ben had left, Marcia pointed at the milk, which had been left out on the table. "Should I just leave it out?"

I nodded. "And don't clean anything up, either." I glanced at the clock and hurriedly opened a can of cat food for Czar Nicholas, who was rubbing against my legs and meowing impatiently. "I've got to start getting up earlier," I said. "Either that or . . . ." It was then that the idea came to me, in a blinding flash. "Marcia!" I shouted, as she was about to go out the back door. "Wait!" It was Dad who'd said it.

Going to school was our work. "What does one union do to show support for another?"

Marcia shrugged and checked the clock. "They refuse to cross picket lines?"

"Yes, but what else?"

"Jenny, I've got to go!"

"Just think about it. What else do they do?"

"Well, sometimes they go on a sympathy strike."

"Right! That's what we'll do. We'll go on strike, too."

"But isn't that what we're already doing, sort of? Like not putting the milk away?"

"Don't you remember what Dad said about our work? He said we shouldn't have to do a lot of housework because the work of children was to go to school."

Marcia raised her eyebrows. "You don't mean . . . ."

"Of course I do. If Mom can stop doing her work, why can't we stop doing ours?"

"Oh, Jenny, I couldn't! What about my report? What about my math test?"

I scraped the last of the cat food out of the can and threw the can into the waste basket. "You don't have to, of course. But it would be better if we did it together."

Marcia set her lunch and her book bag on the table. "Do you really mean you're going to skip school today?"

"And every day as long as Mom's on strike."

"But Jenny, that's illegal. We *have* to go to school."

There were plenty of kids in my school who didn't come every day. Some of them were hardly ever there, and nobody ever seemed to do anything about it. "They say that," I assured her, "but I don't think they really do anything if you don't. And anyway, we don't go to school when we're sick, and Mom never sends in a note until we go back. I was out for a whole week with the flu last year, and we never bothered to tell anyone until afterwards."

Marcia shifted from foot to foot and glanced at the clock again.

"If you don't decide right away, you're going to be late and ruin your record." Marcia has never been late for school in her life. It's a compulsion that goes with neatness. It's also what convinced her. Better to skip school altogether than to get a tardy mark on her report card.

I put the teakettle back on the stove. "We might as well have a cup of cocoa. Then we can go out and see Mom. We might be the only support she has today." I hoped Mom wouldn't send us to school, but I wasn't sure. I felt the need of something hot, like cocoa, to strengthen my nerve.

Marcia put her lunch in the refrigerator and we took our cocoa into the dining room, where we wouldn't have the clock constantly reminding us that it was time for school and we weren't going.

"Dad's going to be furious," Marcia warned, blowing on a spoonful of her cocoa.

"He isn't going to know," I said. "I'm not crazy!"

"Then how will it help Mom's strike?"

"I'm not sure it will help the strike. But if we tell Dad, he'll just make us go back, and that'll be that. I just want to do something to show Mom that we're on her side. Hardly anyone else is any more."

"What'll I do about math?"

"The same thing you'd do if you were sick. You'll make it up later. Anyway, you do well enough at school. Missing a few days won't hurt."

"I hope not."

I wasn't sure Marcia would stay on strike, but at least she was stuck for one day. After that, we could take it a day at a time. Of course, if Mom told us to, we'd both have to go back.

When we finally got the nerve to go out to the front yard, a woman we didn't know was walking the picket line, wearing a ski jacket, a muffler and mittens. It was damp and windy and miserable out there. She nodded as we headed for the tent, and we nodded back. The second tent had disappeared, leaving only a yellow patch on the grass where it had been.

I hadn't talked to Mom in more than a week and was a little scared, so I let Marcia go in first. Someone had loaned Mom a kerosene heater, and it really worked. Buffy was stretched out in the middle of the cot and Mom was sitting at a small table with a steaming cup of coffee, writing something. She looked up, grinned, and then frowned. "Wait a minute," she said, looking at me. "I'll get it. Just a minute. Jenny, isn't it? Marcia's older sister?"

"Very funny," I said. "Very funny, coming from some strange radical who took my mother's place."

Mom looked at her watch and then back at us. "Is this some sort of holiday I don't know about?"

Marcia jabbed me with her elbow, so I swallowed the enormous lump in my throat and spoke, my voice quavering just a little in spite of my determination to be casual. "We've joined the strike," I said. "Dad says school is our work, so we've stopped going to school."

Mom didn't say anything, but she tilted her head at Marcia, as if asking her something.

"Me too," Marcia said.

"In spite of your report?"

Marcia swallowed, too. "I think *because* of it."

I waited for Mom to order us back to school. But she didn't. For a minute, she didn't move, didn't say anything. Then she stood up and held out her arms. As if we were both about Amy's age, Marcia and I rushed into her arms and the three of us stood there in the warmth of the heater and hugged each other.

"I want you to be sure of this, though," Mom said, sitting back down at the table. "If you do it, it's your responsibility, and you'll have to take whatever consequences there may be."

We both nodded. Then we shoved Buffy off the cot and sat down.

"Did you meet Tina outside?" Mom asked. "She's one of the few people left in my poor little organization. She doesn't have children. My other most faithful colleague is Arlene Morrow. She went to the Shell station for a minute, but she'll be back. Her kids are both teenagers and she says nobody on earth could criticize her for abandoning *them!*"

"I'm sorry the rest of them quit," I said.

Mom took a sip of her coffee and then laughed. "I was upset at first. I'm still upset about that travesty of a newspaper story. But I should have known better than to think I could change the whole world. Better women than I have been trying for years."

"So are you going to quit?" Marcia asked.

Mom shook her head. "Do I look like a quitter? I may not be Bella Abzug or Betty Friedan, but I'm not a marshmallow either. Just because I can't change the whole world, doesn't mean I can't do something about my own family. I meant it when I said I wouldn't come back until we can talk about making some changes. I'm not going to be everybody's servant—ever again. We'll *all* be better off that way. I really believe that." She stared over our heads then for a moment, seeming to be thinking about something totally else. "How's Rick doing?" she asked. "Is he remembering to take his lunch? And his jacket? Is anybody tucking him in at night?"

I looked at Marcia and she looked back at me. We'd thought about his lunches, but as far as we knew, he'd been going to bed on his own. We'd forgotten that he was still little enough to want Mom to tuck him in every night—when she was with us. "Dad probably is," I said. But I didn't *really* think that.

"And how's Ben's solar project coming?"

"I think he quit on that," Marcia said.

"Oh. I'm sorry. Is he still furious at me?"

If there was one thing Ben was besides embarrassed, I guessed it had to be "furious." We both nodded.

I thought Mom was going to ask another question, about Dad maybe, but she didn't. She just stared off again, and then patted Buffy's head. "Poor Buffy. All that attention she's been getting, and now there's hardly anybody left."

"Czar Nicholas is the one I feel sorry for," Marcia said. "He's in the house all alone every day without Buffy to play with. No chases, no pouncing on Buffy's tail, no fun at all!"

"He'll live," Mom said. "Cats are very adaptable. Like people."

We spent the rest of the day with Mom and her friends. She wouldn't let us walk the picket line, for fear we'd get our pictures taken and people would say she was encouraging truancy. She said if the press got any worse, she was likely to get lynched. Tina, Arlene, and Mom took turns on the picket line, while the rest of us played cards. Tina had been around the world a couple of times before she got married. She told us wild stories about a month with some maharishi in India and the years she spent in the Peace Corps. Arlene hadn't had such an adventurous life, but she could tell about washing diapers in the bathroom sink when she and her husband were in college so that it seemed like the funniest thing that had ever happened to anybody.

Almost before we knew it, it was time for Rick to come home, and Mom sent us back to the house. We had decided not to tell anyone we were skipping school unless they noticed. We didn't know how long that would take, but in the meantime, there was no sense risking a big fight.

The only person who noticed that day was Sarah. She came over to find out if I was sick and when I told her what we were doing, even Sarah the radical feminist was impressed. "Jeez, I wish I could join you," she said. "But if there's one thing Rachel puts above feminism, it's education. It's the only Jewish tradition she hasn't given up."

That night we tried our first sabotage operation. Ben had a late soccer practice, so he wasn't home in time to help with dinner. Dad asked Marcia to cut up some hot dogs into one of the pots of baked beans, and me to make a salad. Rick was to set the table while Dad, grumbling the whole time, cleaned up the mess from breakfast. Marcia put the beans on at the highest heat.

It wasn't so easy to sabotage a salad, but I was pretty proud of the way I managed it. I found a recipe for curry salad dressing. Now, I happen to like curry. So does Mom— that's why we have it in the house. But everybody else hates it—*hates* it! Later, I suggested that it must have been the stress of being temporarily motherless that made me forget that.

Ben got home to find a dinner of badly scorched beans and franks, curried salad, and milk that had gone sour from sitting out all day. The minute he got inside the door, Dad sent him back out on his bike to 7-Eleven for milk. I think everybody settled for peanut butter and jelly sandwiches that night. I, at least, had a nice salad with mine.

Afterwards, I reminded Marcia about Rick's getting tucked into bed. Even if he was part of the enemy, he was still pretty little, after all. So she suggested to Dad that maybe he should do it. Dad shrugged—it hadn't occurred to him before—and went upstairs. But when he came back down, he was frowning. "I don't know what you two are so worried about," he said. "Rick says he's too big to be tucked in! He says Superman doesn't get tucked in."

The weird thing was that when I went up a while later to do my homework, I thought I heard Rick crying. But his door was closed and I didn't think Superman would want to be caught crying right after he'd made a big deal about being so grown up, so I didn't go in.

The next morning Marcia and I got up at the regular time and got dressed as if we were going to school. We went through the morning cereal ritual, too, even though we knew that Mom and Tina and Arlene were having pancakes outside. Rick forgot to fix himself a lunch again, so Dad gave him another two dollars. "But this is positively the last time!" he warned.

Ben was the last to pour himself cereal, and I kicked Marcia under the table when he put the milk on the counter instead of back in the refrigerator.

"Do you have soccer practice again tonight?" Dad asked. Ben nodded. Since the potluck supper, he had gone from Committed Soldier back to Hermit again, coming and going without talking to anybody, and spending most of his time in his room. It was too cold for the garage. The noises from his room, though, suggested that he'd moved most of his workshop inside. "Well, I hope you can get home sooner tonight than last night," Dad said. "It wouldn't hurt you to help with dinner now and then."

Ben didn't say anything to that, either. He just finished his cereal, grabbed his books and left. The door slammed behind him.

When Rick started out the door, Dad stopped him. "It's forty degrees outside," he said. "Where's your jacket?"

Rick shrugged. "I must have left it somewhere," he said.

"Don't you *know*?" Rick shrugged again. "Didn't you notice you were cold coming home yesterday?"

"Nope."

"Well, find another jacket, then. You can't go to school in this weather like that."

But there wasn't another jacket. Dad sent him up to find a sweat shirt, and then ended up driving him to school.

When they'd left, Marcia pointed to the milk on the counter. We wondered how long it would take before somebody caught on.

We spent another day in the tent. This time, Tina had brought a chess set and offered to teach us all to play. "Not enough girls learn how to play chess," she said. "And if you two aren't going to be in school, you ought to be learning something worthwhile." According to Tina, chess was probably more worthwhile than anything we'd have learned in school anyway. Tina didn't like schools. Or banks. Or churches. Or cities. After two years in the Peace Corps, she didn't like the Peace Corps either. It was probably a good thing Wives/MAD had shrunk. If it had gotten really big, and if it had succeeded in making great changes, Tina wouldn't have liked Wives/MAD either.

Marcia and I stayed on strike the rest of the week. She cheated a little by calling a friend for her assignments and keeping up with her homework in between chess lessons. But I was proud of her. It isn't easy for someone like Marcia to break even little rules, let alone an actual law. Besides, she'd seen Juvenile Hall. We went on with our sabotage strategy, messing up everything we did or forgetting to do things altogether. But by the weekend, we were beginning to get worried. The more we goofed up, the better everybody else got. After his third trip to 7-Eleven to replace sour milk, Ben made sure everything was put away in the morning before he left for school. He even checked to see if we needed eggs or bread or something and started a list which he stuck to the refrigerator with a magnet, so Dad would remember to pick things up on his way home from work. After Marcia and I forgot to run the dishwasher two nights in a row, Dad got so he'd check it before he went to bed at night. Even Rick was getting good at making salads and cleaning up the kitchen.

The weekend presented a problem. With Dad home from work and the boys home from school, we couldn't forget to do things and I couldn't very well do a bad job on the laundry, when I'd done it so well the week before. Dad was making plans for a big cleaning day on Saturday so he could take Sunday off.

It was Sarah's mother who solved the problem. She invented some "old" plans we had made to go camping together in the mountains before the fall foliage season was over. She even called Dad and explained that Sarah and her sister would be heartbroken if Marcia and I couldn't go. It just shows how little Dad knew about us that he fell for the story. Sarah's sister is sixteen and she doesn't even speak to *me*, let alone Marcia. In fact, she's such a pain that I don't usually even sleep over at Sarah's unless Mimi's going to be away.

The funny thing was that we really did go camping, and even with Mimi along, we all had a super time. The weather was still chilly, but the sun kept coming out between the clouds on Saturday when we were on our six-mile hike, so we could sit and rest in the sun, sometimes, to get warm. It was so much fun that we forgot all about the strike. On Sunday morning we stopped at a pick-them-yourself orchard and picked a bushel of apples for each family.

When we got back that evening, we dropped some apples off at Mom's tent and went inside. Dad was watching a football game, Rick was creating an elaborate space station with Legos, and Ben had gone to a games arcade with his friend Mark. But the house looked good. When we went to put our camping stuff away, we saw that the laundry had been done and our clothes were stacked neatly on our beds. "They even did the bathrooms," Marcia said when she came back to our room. "And smell that! Dad must be making Mom's oven stew."

It was definitely scary. If companies could get along without strikers, the strikers were simply out of a job. I imagined Mom still out in the tent when the snow started. And if we didn't go back to school eventually, we'd never catch up! What had started out as a strike was really getting to seem more and more like the war Dad had called it in the first place. With the enemies so far apart and so determined to win, it was beginning to seem as if we'd never get to the bargaining table—or the peace table—to begin negotiations. I was beginning to wonder if both sides had dug their trenches too deep to climb out of.

But as we sat on our beds and worried that night, we forgot that there are differences between companies—or armies—and families. Even later, on my way to the bathroom, when I saw Dad standing at the hall window looking down at the front yard, as I'd seen him doing several times in the past week, I didn't think of it. The other thing I didn't think of was the compulsory education law.

NEGOTIATION

Meanwhile, behind the scenes and unbeknownst to our hero [me], *evil forces were at work.*

This is the good part about telling a story later—you know things you weren't aware of at the time. Marcia and I might not have known much about the compulsory education law, but there were plenty of other people who did.

When you hear about kids playing hooky, there is always the figure of the truant officer lurking around in a sinister way. I used to visualize this person as a man with a uniform, and a hat like a Canadian mountie's, who goes around to all the neat places kids might hang out if they weren't in school. He rounds them up, almost like a dog catcher with a net, and takes them back to school by the scruff of the neck.

There is no such person in our town. Instead, there's the truancy board. If a kid misses more than five consecutive days of school without an excuse, the case can be turned over to the truancy board. The board can take whatever action it thinks fits the case, but usually starts out with a phone call to the kid's parents. Sometimes the phone call is enough and nothing else ever happens. But if the kid still doesn't go back to school, there are other things the board can do. The last resort, when every other tactic has failed, is to turn the case over to the courts and prosecute the parents. It almost never goes that far. Besides that, the truancy board hardly ever gets a case after the minimum number of absences. Usually somebody has to miss more like a month before the board gets into it. That's *usually*.

The day after Marcia and I had missed our fifth day, both our cases got sent to the truancy board. Somebody may have tried to call our house that day, but I wouldn't guarantee it. The truancy board is made up entirely of men, and they are men who read the newspapers. Here were two cases—two girls—named Skinner. So the board chose to exercise its option and act—immediately. Skipping right to the last of its possibilities. If you think the law is upheld with an even hand, you can think again!

It was Thursday, October 20. Marcia and I had spent most of the day learning about Buddhism from Tina. She says all Westerners ought to learn about all Eastern religions, and vice versa. She says understanding the minds and cultures of one's fellow humans is the only hope for the future of the world. Actually, Tina doesn't have much hope for the future of the world, but she says she does what she can.

As usual, we went back to the house "after school." We got the mail from the mailbox as we went inside and put it at Dad's place at the table without looking at it. Since we never get anything, we never pay attention to the mail.

When Dad got home from work, we were all in the kitchen getting ready for dinner. Ben was basting the chicken he was roasting from a recipe he said was super easy, Marcia was setting the table, Rick was doing his now-regular job of making the salad, and I was trying to decide whether or not to sabotage the vegetables again. Dad said hi, fixed himself a drink (a new habit he'd picked up P.S.) and took the mail and newspaper into the family room. The television went on, the news started, and the only other sound from the family room was the gentle rustling of the newspaper. There was a distinct (and erroneous) sense of domestic tranquility in the scene.

I had decided that I couldn't come up with a subtle way to damage a perfectly straightforward can of spinach, and anyway, I wasn't sure I could stand another wrecked meal, when a sound like the bellow of an enraged bull seemed to shake the foundations of the house. Unfortunately, I had already opened the spinach and Marcia had just taken the new gallon jug of milk out of the refrigerator and opened it. Thinking back, it's hard to decide what happened first, but somehow Czar Nicholas got tangled in Marcia's legs just as Marcia, startled by the enraged bull sound, let go of the milk. That was about the time that I, instead of just dropping the can of spinach, must have tossed in into the air. At least, when it came down, it was no longer right side up. Czar Nicholas, Marcia, the milk, and the spinach all got sort of mixed together on the floor.

A large gray Persian cat drenched with milk, festooned with spinach, and terrified out of his mind, is a formidable opponent in a wrestling match, even an accidental one. By the time Dad's voice had translated itself into actual human language, Marcia had a deep scratch across one cheek and I had an entire set of claw marks down the arm I had gallantly reached out to help disentangle them. In the melee I remember hearing Dad shout for Marcia and me to come to the family room, but I didn't hear the doorbell that must have rung at just about the same moment. In fact, Rick was the only person who heard the doorbell, and he says it rang

three times before he figured no one else was going to answer
it, so he'd better.

Meantime, Marcia and I were making our way in the direction of the family room, tracking milk and spinach and
beginning to drip blood from the wounds caused by our now-
vanished cat. Ben, with morbid curiosity, was following us.
Marcia kept doing her best to stay behind me, while I was
trying to make myself small enough to get behind her, so it
wasn't a particularly graceful entrance.

Dad was standing where he had jumped up out of his chair,
an official-looking typed letter in his hand. On the floor in
front of him were the newspaper and the rest of the mail,
scattered in a rough semicircle around his feet. "I would
like an explanation!" he yelled, Clint Eastwood with a
megaphone.

Meanwhile, Rick had gone to the door and, innocently
enough, had opened it. Czar Nicholas, who had taken refuge
under the couch in the living room, saw his chance and
bolted through the door, crashing into the woman who was
standing on the porch and leaving splatters of green on the
skirt of her suit as he scrambled between her legs. For a
moment, the woman apparently considered abandoning her
mission. She backed down the porch steps, wiping ineffec-
tually at her skirt. Rick thinks it was the thundery sound of
Dad's voice asking for an explanation that changed her mind,
because right after that she came back up and introduced
herself. Rick isn't very good at introductions or figuring out
what adults want from him, so he decided he'd better just
take her in to talk to Dad. Leaving the front door open, he
led the way to the family room.

In crisis situations there are certain central issues that

take up everybody's attention, and side issues that tend to get ignored. Rick and the woman who appeared in the doorway were, to Dad, mere side issues. By the time they arrived, he was well into his dramatic reading of the letter, which was, as we'd guessed, from the truancy board. The letter threatened to take Mom and Dad to court and explained that the penalty for violating the compulsory education law could include a jail term for the parents. It could also include making the children wards of the state, if the social service agency recommended such an action.

It can be a very good thing in a situation like that to get mad, because when you're mad, you don't have room to be scared at the same time. "What's going on in this family is our business," Marcia said. "It has nothing to do with the school system or the truancy board or anybody else!"

"Besides," I added, "the kids who miss school all the time in my class don't get taken away from their parents because of it. And their parents don't get sent to jail. It doesn't take an Einstein to figure there's somebody who doesn't like the idea of women on strike!"

"What has this got to do with the strike?" Dad asked, his voice still sounding as if it was coming through a megaphone.

"We're on strike, too. You said school was our work. So this is a sympathy strike," Marcia said.

"A what?"

"A sympathy strike," I said, and wished my voice hadn't begun to quiver that way.

"Didn't you know skipping school is against the law?"

"But nobody takes kids away from their parents for it. They can't *do* that!" Marcia said.

"I'm afraid they can." This came from the woman with the spinach on her skirt. She came the rest of the way into the room and stood for a moment, looking at Marcia, taking in the bloody streak across her cheek, her milk-wet hair plastered against her forehead, the spinach on her shirt and jeans. Then she looked pointedly at the scratches on my arm, and back at Dad. "I'm Janet Norton, your social worker," she said.

"We don't have a social worker," Dad said.

"I'm afraid you do now. I have been assigned to investigate the family situation and make recommendations should the truancy case come to court."

As if on some diabolical cue, Buffy and Czar Nicholas decided at that moment to renew their relationship. Apparently, Czar Nicholas had taken cover in Mom's tent, where he was spotted by Buffy, who was delighted to have her old playmate back again and gave chase. Czar Nicholas appeared first, hissing and spitting as he ran, and dashed between Dad and the social worker, curving around them to leap onto the back of Dad's chair. Buffy, close on her tail, was too big to take the curve. She skidded violently on the newspaper and crashed into the table, upsetting it and Dad's drink. A cloud of bourbon smell wafted into the air.

I remember at least one scream, a great deal of barking, Dad yelling, and the television—oblivious to everything— going on about the joys of diet cola, before things got sorted out. Ben finally caught Buffy and shoved her out the front door, Rick and Marcia shooed Czar Nicholas into the living room, staying carefully away from his claws, and I sopped up the drink with paper towels. Dad was doing his best to summon his Ward Cleaver self and get the situation under control.

When we were all back, Dad asked the social worker, now very red in the face and clutching the strap of her shoulder bag, to sit down on the couch—as far as he could get her from his chair and the smell of bourbon. His voice sounded almost normal as he asked her to explain her presence more fully.

"In cases of continued truancy," she began, her voice as tight as her grip on her purse, "a social worker is sent to investigate the family situation. We often find that severe family problems underlie a child's prolonged absence from school." She looked around the room, then she glanced at us and shook her head. "Apparently, I arrived at a moment of great *strain*."

"Apparently." Dad made an effort at a smile, but it didn't really make it. "You arrived, actually, at the precise moment that I learned of the school situation for the first time. Do you know how long the 'continued truancy' has gone on in the case of my daughters?"

"As a matter of fact," the woman said, with a kind of icy smile that was no more convincing than Dad's, "I wasn't given the full particulars of the case. It was considered vital that I make my investigation *as soon as possible*. I'm afraid I didn't make the connection between the family name and the . . . um. . . ."—she pursed her lips as if she'd taken a bite of something unpleasant—"the *Skinner strike*."

"If that's true, you seem to be the only one who failed to make the connection. My daughters have missed school for. . . ." He looked at me. "How long?"

"Eight days. Or nine."

"Let's say nine. Is it usual to send a social worker to investigate a family after nine absences?"

"Actually, we *are* more likely to be called in after thirty or forty absences," the woman admitted. "But perhaps the— well—the fairly *public* family problem here led to the de-

termination that an immediate investigation was necessary."
The woman took a deep, shuddering breath that ended with
a slight choking sound. "Excuse me, does that cat sometimes
sleep on this couch?"

"Sometimes?" Rick said. "That's practically *his* couch!"

She took another breath. "I am allergic to cat fur!"

"What a shame," Dad said. "Is there anything we can do?"

"No. No. As long as the cat isn't actually *in* the room—
but it would be best to get this over quickly."

"My feelings exactly," Dad said. He waved his arm around,
indicating us and the room and the house in general. "Re-
gardless of the 'moment of great strain' you happened to
interrupt—a moment that has certain obvious justifications—
what does the situation look like to you? Do these children
look undernourished? Improperly housed? Poorly clothed?
Abused?" He glanced at our now-dried bloody scratches.
"Except by their cat? And what conclusions do you draw
from the fact that of four children only two, the girls, have
been skipping school?" Dad's face was beginning to get a
little pink. Ward Cleaver was fast losing ground.

"Mr. Skinner," the woman said, her voice firm and official-
sounding between gasps, "I don't know exactly what this
strike of your wife's . . . and of your daughters' . . . is all
about. . . . I do know that such a public display . . . of
family . . . *disunity* . . . can have a very serious adverse
effect . . . on the delicate psyches of the children. While
it may not be . . . absolutely necessary for you and your
wife . . . to solve this problem you're having, it *is* . . .
necessary that you assure me that the girls . . . will return
. . . to school . . . tomorrow." She leaned over and tried
to breathe deeply.

"Then there is no reason for us to prolong this interview.

You have my assurances that Jenny and Marcia will both be in school in the morning."

I sighed. Obviously, our sympathy strike had failed. But Marcia, with more courage than I could imagine, more courage than was probably good for her, spoke up. "I'm not going back to school!"

Dad just looked at her. "Of course you are," he said finally.

"No. This is a sympathy strike. If Mom gets the negotiations she asked for, I'll go back. If not, I won't."

I was impressed. I couldn't let Marcia stand alone, Sarah would never forgive me. So I nodded. It wasn't much, but it was all I could manage at the moment.

I don't know what Dad would have done if Janet Norton hadn't been sitting there watching him. I was actively suppressing my natural tendency to create mental pictures, for fear I would collapse under the strain. Anyway, Janet Norton *was* there. "I am your father and I am ordering you to go back to school. Tomorrow!"

I reached out and took Marcia's hand. It was an unaccustomed big-sisterly thing to do, but I figured we both needed the support. She squeezed my hand and said, "No. We can't. And we won't. You can't make that order stick. If you took us to the door, you couldn't make us go in. If you took us right inside, you couldn't make us stay there."

Dad's patient tone of voice was about as convincing as his fatherly smile. "Marcia, there is a law. The truancy board is threatening us with a lawsuit, which would be a terrible inconvenience, to say nothing of the expense. It could get us jailed. You could wind up in Juvenile Hall again."

"Again?" Janet Norton looked for all the world like an animal pricking up its ears.

"It was a mistake. An officer made a mistake."

It was time for me to get my voice under control and support my little sister. "Marcia and I decided to support Mom's strike, and we haven't changed our minds."

Dad's face was now an ominous shade of red, a shade that seemed to grow deeper as I watched. He stood up, slowly, and it was as if I'd been hypnotized. I couldn't take my eyes off him. "You are children," he thundered, no longer concerned about the social worker's presence. *"My children! And you will do what you're told!"*

Marcia shook her head. I shook mine.

"Mr. Skinner," Janet Norton said, "It is obvious to me that there is a serious lack of . . . parental authority in this family." She gasped and wheezed and wiped at her watering eyes. "I will give you until Monday to have all your children in school . . . or I will have to make a *negative* recommendation . . . a *strongly* negative recommendation."

"There is no lack of parental authority in this family!" Dad shouted.

It was then that Czar Nicholas, having cleaned the spinach off his fur, came to join the group. Before anyone had noticed his presence, he leaped lightly into Ms. Norton's lap, his tail high.

I have heard about people cracking up, but this was the first time I had ever seen it. Rick said later he thought someone had thrown a hand grenade. Janet Norton leaped from the couch, screaming hysterically and hurling a startled Czar Nicholas to the floor. Words could be understood only intermittently. I managed to catch "filthy beast" and "madhouse" and "crazy people" before the gasping took over entirely. As she bent over, clutching her shoulder bag to her stomach, apparently trying to get a breath, I saw her aim a kick in the general direction of Czar Nicholas, who was by this time standing with his back arched and his fur on end, spitting at someone he clearly took to be a deadly enemy.

"Don't touch that cat!" Dad shouted. "And get out of my house! We don't need any interference from social agencies here!"

"I'm going," Janet Norton gasped, as she headed for the front door. "But you haven't heard the last of me!" A choking fit overcame her as she tried to open the door, and then she was outside on the front porch. "I know all about you people!" she shrieked. She wiped at her streaming eyes. "Hiding behind your middle-class disguise! Letting your children run wild! Drinking! Who knows what else!"

Mom came out of the tent with Buffy at her heels.

"Keep that animal away from me!" the social worker screamed. "I know all about you, too. Living in a tent. Dragging motherhood in the dirt!"

We had all followed the woman into the front yard and stood watching as Janet Norton, still gasping and muttering, flung herself into her car and took off with a great screeching of tires.

"What was all that about?" Mom asked.

"That madwoman thinks she's going to take the children away from us," Dad said.

Before she could respond, Rick pointed to the open front door. "Smoke!" he yelled. "The house is on fire!"

Sure enough, a thin wisp of smoke was floating out the door. "My chicken!" Ben shrieked, and was through the door before anyone else could move.

That was how the Skinner family, all of it, ended up in the kitchen together exactly seventeen days after the be-

ginning of the Great Skinner Strike. In fact, it wasn't until
Ben had taken the smoking, blackened remains of his
chicken out of the oven and we'd mopped up the milk and
spinach that we fully realized the significance of that fact.

"Well," Mom said, looking around her. "Here we are."

"Yes. Here we are," Dad said.

They stood looking at each other awkwardly, and I was
reminded of the way Sarah and I act when we've had a
really terrible argument and neither of us knows who should
apologize and who should forgive.

"That was supposed to be your dinner?" Mom asked.

Ben nodded. "It would have been good, too!"

"Have you eaten?" Dad asked.

"Not yet," Mom said.

"Well . . ."—he looked at us—"can we come up with a
meal we can share?"

Half an hour later, we put on the table a dinner composed
of Dad's ham and cheese omelette, Rick's salad, and a can
of beets I heated up, when we'd all agreed not to try again
with spinach. Marcia had finished setting the table while
Ben disappeared into the bathroom, coming out only when
the food was ready, his face looking like the sky before a
thunderstorm. While we worked, Mom sat on the kitchen
stool out of the way, with Czar Nicholas purring contentedly
in her lap. It was as if she were a guest.

When we finished eating a meal consumed mostly in a
kind of embarrassed silence, Rick pushed himself away from
the table and without a word climbed into Mom's lap. He
nestled his head against her shoulder, and you'd never believe he had invented any story about a wicked stepmother.
And Mom didn't seem to be a guest any more.

"What's this about taking the children away?" she asked.

So Dad explained what Janet Norton had said. And Marcia repeated our determination to continue our strike. Dad's face began to take on a tinge of pink again, and Mom turned to Marcia.

"Thank you, Marcia. You, too, Jenny. But it's possible to take even a good thing too far. It's time to go back to school."

Marcia looked at me, and I shrugged. What I really felt was relief. I didn't think I'd be any good at standing up to a violent father. Marcia was probably relieved too, but she was too stubborn to let it show. "But your strike—" she began.

"—is *my* strike. If your support of it jeopardizes this family, do you really want to continue to support it?"

We shook our heads.

"I didn't think so. After all, we can't have family negotiations if we don't have a *family*."

"*Do* we have a family?" Dad asked. I didn't hear Ward Cleaver *or* Clint Eastwood. Just Michael Skinner. And he sounded tired.

Mom patted Rick's back and looked at Ben and Marcia and me. "Do we?" Everyone but Ben nodded. At almost thirteen, I guess it's hard to give up Clint Eastwood.

"Then can we have negotiations?" She sounded tired too.

Dad frowned at the remains of the food on the table, and then at us. "The truth is," he said at last, "we've all learned something. Not just how to mop a floor, but how much there is to keeping it mopped—and us fed—and the clothes clean. *Some* of what you asked for makes sense."

"Some of it?"

"You don't expect a total surrender, do you? Whatever happened to 'negotiations'?"

"All right. All in favor, say 'aye.'"

Ben refused to open his mouth, and Rick, his head still on Mom's shoulder, had fallen asleep. Still, the "ayes" had it.

"Can we consider the strike—both strikes—suspended while we negotiate?" Dad asked.

Mom and Marcia and I nodded. "I'll take Rick up to bed," Mom said. "And then I could use some help bringing things in from the front yard."

"I'll do the dishes," Ben said, and took his plate to the sink. One member of the family was still at war.

AFTERWORD

Marcia and I went back to school the next day, and the truancy board dropped the case. We never saw Janet Norton again, but Czar Nicholas hasn't been near the couch in the family room ever since.

It took more than a week of negotiations, but we finally came up with a contract everybody was willing to sign. Mom's chart was every bit as powerful as Marcia had thought it would be. We went over every one of Mom's demands, and she finally got them all, one way or another, because it turned out that it wouldn't just be Mom who'd be better off that way. She kept reminding us that underneath everything was the need to respect each other, and that sharing didn't just mean the work, but the good things, too.

Ben rejoined the family and signed the contract when he was guaranteed several things. One was that part of the family's income would go to pay for raw materials

for his building projects. Another was
that his workshop area and his time to use
it would be protected. And finally, he
wouldn't be the only one asked to make
emergency trips to 7-Eleven anymore.
Everyone would have to take turns doing
that.

Marcia and I got our own rooms. Ben and
Rick didn't have to move in together,
either. I'll get Rick's room and Ben and
Dad are fixing a room in the attic for
Rick, complete with a combination bunk
bed/clubhouse Ben's designing.

It turned out that there are a whole
bunch of jobs nobody wanted to do at all,
like cleaning out the litter box. Those
were handed out on a rotating basis.
Otherwise, everybody has specific job
assignments. And there are to be regular
family conferences where anyone who has a
gripe can talk about it. Everybody gets
bigger allowances, partly because Mom has
taken a full-time job as research assistant
to a writer she met at the library. And
everyone gets to control his or her own
money. (Rick's first allowance went for a
whole case of snack cakes, but after that
night in the bathroom, he decided to put
his money in a bank instead.)

At first it seemed as if Dad was the
only one who didn't get anything in the
new scheme of things, except that there's

enough money now to send his shirts out to
be washed and ironed. But when Sarah and
I came in from the library the other night,
Mom and Dad were necking by the kitchen
sink. So I guess there are some things
about the end of the strike that have
nothing to do with contracts. I don't
think Sarah understands about that part.

We drank a bottle of champagne to
celebrate the signing of the contract, and
Marcia says Mom won. I'm not so sure,
though. The old way had lasted an awfully
long time. We have a contract, all right.
But in a family, nobody can be fired,
whether the contract is kept or not. And
even though there are plenty of Protestants
around, which shows that somebody did
something about the Ninety-five Theses,
the Catholic Church is still pretty big.
And pretty powerful.

One thing I know for sure. The Skinners
are no longer a normal middle-class
family. I also know that for the purpose
of telling the kids' side of the Great
Skinner Strike, this book is over. But
only books end. Real stories go right on.